For

LESBIAN SE
MÓNIC

Close Your Eyes

"Well, Rachel, I'm afraid the x-rays show what we already feared, both your arms are broken, I'm very sorry"

I nodded and tilted my head to one side without saying anything, what good would it do me? Unless someone had arms to spare, no one could help me. I suppose deep down I had to be grateful because if that ceiling lamp had hit me in the head instead of my arms when it fell on my desk, I wouldn't be telling this story now.

After the nurse had put a cast on my arms and healed the wounds the glass had left on my hands, the doctor signed me out and I took a taxi to take me home. Along the way, I was thinking about how I was going to manage on my own with practically no use of my hands. I could move my fingers, but they hurt a lot, and in addition to the cuts I had a lot of bruises from the impact.

I think anyone else in my situation would have felt hopeless, but I was so used to being alone and not being able to count on anyone, that I guess that condition didn't scare me as much as it should have.

I was more worried about the anxiety and loneliness I was feeling than the fact of not having arms for a month. It had been three weeks since my company had transferred me to the Valencia office, they needed to fill a position with a temporary worker who already had experience and what better candidate than a single woman, with no children and no plans to have a family, because I didn't even have a pet.

I accepted without giving it much thought, after all it wasn't that far from Madrid, I would have gone to visit my parents once a month and that was it. My best friend had just got married and I didn't have much time for myself, so there was nothing to keep me there.

I think that before arriving home, I had already planned how I would have done it all. I only found two things that I knew I couldn't have done on my own: the first one, to fasten or unfasten my bra, and the second one, to wash my head. For the first one, the only solution I could think of was not to put it on, after all, in my condition I would have hardly gone out of the house, and I never wore it there. For the second one, there was only one option, to go to a hairdresser's and have my head washed. I had already planned how to wash my body and, although I knew it was going to be much more difficult than I thought, I was sure that with a little patience I would have managed to do it, and well, if there was one thing I was going to have during that month, it was time.

But the head thing was very complicated, the mere fact of raising my arms made me rage with pain. There were too many things, washing my head, soaping, rinsing and untangling. No, no way, I couldn't, and even less if I had to avoid getting my casts wet.

That evening I took off my bra and pulled it down to my waist and never wore it again. I writhed in pain to get my trousers off, I had to juggle to get my dinner ready, and putting a single bite in my mouth became a living hell. My hands were shaking with pain and the plaster cast prevented me from closing my arm completely. With great care and effort, I managed to grasp the fork with two fingers, but I was in so much pain that I had to let go before I could get the food in my mouth. I even considered the option of eating the macaroni like a dog, straight from the plate, but the very despair of the situation killed my appetite, so I ended up drinking a glass of milk through a straw. Even brushing my teeth became a real odyssey for me, and that was just the beginning.

That night I cried again, as I had been doing so often for the past year. I guess you could say I was a little depressed. I was thirty-five years old and I still didn't know what it was like to feel loved, I had never found anyone who could show me what it was like to be cared for, to be missed. Never.

I guess for many years I didn't care, I thought it would have come eventually, but when I turned thirty-five, I hit a slump. If I wasn't able to attract someone who loved me in my best years, how was I supposed to as I got older and my body withered more and more?

During the week that feeling of emptiness and sadness was more bearable, my job kept me distracted and tiredness didn't let me think much. It was at the weekend when I had the worst time, when I realized how lonely I was in that empty house, with no one to talk to or just to go for a walk with. It was a horrible feeling, and now I was going to spend a month locked up at home with no arms and no one to ask for help. Perfect.

It had only been a few hours since my accident and I had already seen how hard it was going to be. The thought of having to spend a month in that state made something inside me shrink, I had never felt so lonely and so sad.

The next morning, after more than an hour to get a shower and having to put on a pair of sweatpants because I couldn't pull up my jeans, I grabbed a short-sleeved T-shirt wide enough to make it easy to put on and went down to the hairdresser's a couple of doors away from my building in slippers, of course, because I couldn't tie my trainers either. I'd never been in before, and it probably wasn't the salon I'd choose in a normal situation, it was too big, too many people, and all that equaled too much noise, which in my condition bothered me a lot, but for a head wash, I would have gone for anything.

"I'm sorry, we are full today" said the girl at the counter.

She was writing something down in a notebook and she didn't even bother to raise her head to look me in the face, I only had time to say hello and she was already kicking me out. I think the contempt and indifference with which she spoke to me, added to the helplessness I felt for not being able to do anything by myself, didn't help my mood at all. I felt tears welling up in my eyes and my chin trembling as I held back the urge to cry. I quickly tried to think of another hairdresser nearby, but I couldn't think of any, I didn't know the neighborhood yet and I didn't feel like walking down the street looking like that, so I decided to go back home and try my luck the next day.

"What was it for?" she asked again without raising her head. "I can give you an appointment another day".

"No need, I just wanted you to wash my fucking head" I whispered quietly as I turned away without her hearing me.

As soon as I did so, I noticed that a woman had just entered and was right behind me, I had to stop in my tracks to avoid hitting her and dodge her so I could get out of there.

"I'm sorry" I whispered.

"Wait" she asked, placing her hand on my belly to stop me.

Her voice sounded so sweet and her gesture was so tender and kind, that when I raised my eyes to look at her, I couldn't stop my tears from flowing. I was so ashamed that I ducked my head again and went to the door to run out of there, but I had a new problem: the door opened inwards! When I got there I just had to push it with my shoulder, but now I couldn't get out unless someone helped me, and that was the last straw for me. I stood in front of the door with my eyes fixed on the floor, as if that position would make the door open by itself. Again this woman appeared at my side with terrible kindness.

"I'll open it for you, don't worry."

I didn't even thank her, I left in a hurry, unable to stop her from coming after me.

"Wait, don't go" she asked me.

I stopped and sat down on the front step of the next doorway and tried to calm down a bit.

"You need to have your head washed, don't you? Is that what I heard?" she asked after crouching down in front of me.

"Yes, but it looks like it's all full" I smiled resignedly as I sniffled.

I guess the fact that someone had taken the trouble to listen to me made me feel better. It was then that I looked at her again and I really saw her, she was a bit older than me, or at least she seemed so. She was also the most beautiful woman I had ever seen in my life. She had a very kind expression on her face and a dark look in her eyes that would take your breath away. Her hair was brown and wavy, perfectly combed, as if she had just come out of the hairdresser's.

"I'll do it."

"What?"

"I'll wash your head" she said.

"But the hairdresser said..."

"That girl isn't a hairdresser, she's an asshole, and as soon as her contract runs out, she's out on the street."

I looked at her in surprise.

"The hair salon is mine, come in with me and when there's a free shampoo basin, I'll wash your hair myself."

"I'm sorry, I don't want you to fire anyone because of me, I think she was very busy with her agenda and..."

"It's not just about you, I assure you, that girl has no manners or attitude to stay in front of the public, it's not something I decided today, I made the decision days ago."

She took a packet of tissues out of her purse, pulled one out and offered it to me. I looked at her gratefully before trying to take it with two fingers that were shaking and hurting too much. I didn't even know how I was going to wipe my tears with it and that made me feel worse.

"Damn, I'm insensitive, I'm sorry, let me help you" she said, taking the tissue from my hands when she saw that I couldn't.

"No..." I spluttered in embarrassment.

"Come on, it's all right, girl, they're just tears, and we all need help at some point. Let yourself be helped, come on."

I sighed deeply and she placed her left hand on my chin and used her right one to wipe my face and eyes with care and kindness I had never experienced before.

"Thank you" I whispered.

"You're welcome. Please, come in with me, let's wash your hair and you'll see how good you'll feel after that."

She helped me up and when she opened the door I felt so overwhelmed to see so many people, I was collapsed, I needed silence and I started to breathe heavily.

"Do you mind if I wait out here?"

"No, I don't mind, but look, that girl has already finished, come with me, I promise we won't take long."

I followed her. In a moment she had everything ready and put the towel over my shoulders. I sat up and leaned back. I was so relieved to feel the coolness of the shampoo basin on my neck.

"Are you okay like this?" she asked with a smile as she walked around me to stand behind.

I nodded and stared at the ceiling as she turned on the tap and started to wet my hair. At that moment I let out one of those sighs that feel like you're going to drown, the ones you get after you've cried a lot. I think I was surprised when it happened and I stirred restlessly, trying to hold on to the chair as if I was afraid, but of course, I couldn't. Then I felt as she put her wet hand on my chin and gently stroked me to calm me down.

"It's OK, don't worry, is the temperature OK?"

I nodded again and she began to lather me up gently. I could feel her fingers softly massaging my head and I couldn't help but shiver when I noticed that she was behind my ears and near the back of my neck. She rinsed me a little and then put some mask in my hair.

"Why don't you close your eyes? Now I'll give you a massage, try to relax, it will make you feel better", she whispered to me."

"I can't" I smiled shyly. "I think I'm afraid of doing it."

It was true, I had never done it because I had the feeling that I would be helpless if I did so, I had always envied all the people who relaxed and enjoyed those massages in quiet peace.

"Well, then leave them open, but try to leave your mind blank, don't think about anything."

"Okay."

I listened to her and tried not to think about anything, but I didn't succeed, because at that moment there was one thing that had taken over my thoughts: her. Luckily, it wasn't an unpleasant thought. I had the feeling that she was giving me more time than she should have, maybe she wanted to make up for the way her employee had treated me, but the truth was that I didn't care, because for the first time in a long time I felt calm and relaxed, even if I was unable to close my eyes. After a while, she began to rinse me off and toweled me dry.

"Come, I'll dry your hair. How do you want it? Loose or up?"

"You'd be doing me a favor if you gave me a high ponytail."

"A ponytail then."

I was very annoyed for the time she was using the hairdryer, I wanted it to end quickly because I craved to hear her voice again, I didn't care what she said, I just wanted her to talk to me.

"Do you live nearby?" she asked as she brushed me.

"A couple of doors down, why?"

"Just curious. I assumed that, given your own condition, you must have been looking for the nearest hairdresser" she said with a smile that I saw through the mirror.

"Yeah, I guess I'm not on my last legs."

"What time do you get up?"

"Excuse me?" I asked in surprise.

"I'm not a stalker if that's what you're thinking, come on, answer."

"I usually get up around seven or so. Why do you want to know?"

She bent down behind me and spoke into my ear as she looked at me through the mirror.

"Because I've noticed that people bother you, I guess you're a bit down and I know what it's like, and I also know how much peace is appreciated at those times. I'll tell you what, I don't open until nine o'clock, come at eight o'clock every day and I'll wash you quietly, you'll see how you'll end up closing your eyes. What do you think?"

"Thank you."

That was all I could say, she had no idea how much that meant to me.

"No worries."

After that she gave me the nicest tail I had ever worn, if it wasn't for my looks, I would have even felt pretty.

"How do you feel now?" she whispered in my ear as she put her arms next to mine and looked at me through the mirror.

It made me so nervous, I loved the way she looked at me and how caring she was.

"Clean" I smiled.

I could see through the mirror the stupid look on my face at my silly answer and how she was smiling and still looking at me.

"Clean and pretty" she said, stroking my tail.

I smiled again and we both headed for the counter.

"How much do I owe you? I have the money in my pocket."

"Nothing" she smiled.

"No way, no way, if you don't charge me, I won't come back."

"Just for today. Any other day you'll pay me, but not today. It's the least I can do after the deal she gave you."

"You've already rewarded me more than enough."

She smiled at me again, and with each new smile, I found it harder to look at her without blushing.

"I'm glad, but it's still on the house today."

"Thank you."

"Hey" she said as I was about to leave.

"What?"

"You'll be all right?"

"Yeah, don't worry" I smiled shily.

I thanked her again and went home, I took advantage of a neighbor going out to cross the doorway and after trying to turn the key to my door with my mouth without success, I had to call another neighbor to open it for me. I didn't realized until I was inside my house that I didn't even know her name, but I didn't care, because the next day I would have seen her again and I could have asked her.

I spent the rest of the day more quietly than I would have imagined, I ordered Chinese food for lunch, some spring rolls, so I didn't have to use cutlery. I spent the afternoon reading and watching series on the laptop to distract myself and not to think about how much I was looking forward to the next day.

I got up a little before seven because I wanted to take a shower, which of course took much longer than usual. That day I wasn't willing to go in the same looks as the day before, so I wore black elastic trousers that were less difficult to pull up by holding them between the casts, but when I managed to do so, I found another problem: the fucking button. I was unable to fasten it, but since I had been able to pull up the zip I thought it would have been enough. For the top I had no choice, a bra was still a no-no and a wide T-shirt was still necessary. Instead of my slippers, I wore sneakers, and as I couldn't fasten the laces, I tucked them on one side so as not to step on them. The last thing that I needed was to fall!

At eight o'clock I stood at the door of the hairdresser's, the shutter was already up and the door open, she was at the back preparing the shampoo basin.

"Hello" I said shyly.

"Hey, hi! Wait, I'll close the door so that no one comes in, go and sit down."

I think I found her even more beautiful that morning than the day before, I felt a terrible tingle and my heart stopped for a few moments when she passed by me and squeezed my arm in an affectionate greeting before closing the door.

She began to soap and massage my head as gently as she had done the day before, but I started to feel little cramps of pleasure run through my body as her fingers dug into my hair. Everything was absolutely silent, there was no noise, no voices, no music, not even the sound of cars, it was so quiet that I could hear her slow, calm and relaxed breathing.

"Am I too indiscreet if I ask what happened to you?"

"No" I smiled. "It was an accident at work, a ceiling light came off and fell on my arms while I was typing on my laptop."

"Wow, that's really bad luck. I think it's the first time I've seen someone with both arms in plaster. Are you doing well? Do you live with someone?"

I smiled before answering, I was sure that this question hid something more than just an interest in knowing if I was doing well on my own.

"I live alone, but I'm getting by."

"Yes, I can see that, you've hidden your shoelaces so as not to step on them" she said teasingly at my smile. "Alright, it's time, close your eyes."

I tried, but as soon as I did it, I was overcome with anxiety and I suddenly opened them again.

"Don't worry. Maybe tomorrow" she whispered.

And I smiled again. She gave me another ponytail and we talked for a while until the first of her employees arrived. After that, she helped me up and we walked together to the counter.

"Wait, let me tie your laces, I don't want you to fall."

"No need, really, I doubt I'll fall from here to my house."

But it was too late, I had already put one knee on the floor to tie my shoelaces.

"Shall I fasten your trousers too? " she asked teasingly.

"Huh?"

I think I ran out of breath. As soon as she asked me that question I looked down at my waist like a robot on command. I guess when I was sitting down the zip must have come down and I hadn't even noticed that, the shirt covered the unfastened button, but not the zip, and my panties were showing, dammit. I turned as red as a tomato and she smiled in amusement.

"Let's see."

She moved behind me and wrapped her arms around me until she reached for the zip, I felt a jolt of excitement in the center of my body as I felt her fingers brush against my waist as she fastened the button, and then struggle to grab the tiny zip puller just above my genitals and pull it up. When she was done, she stayed close to me for a few seconds, as if she needed to feel me. It was for a very brief time, but enough to make me wish she would never leave my side. I suddenly felt a terrible need to have her close to me.

"Well, I think that's it" she announced after clearing her voice.

"Thank you, again."

"You're welcome, again. I'll give you my number if you need anything, okay? I'm just a stone's throw away from your house, so if you need help with anything, just give me a call."

She took a marker pen and started drawing her phone numbers on my left cast.

"So you can't tell me you've lost it" she whispered mischievously at my amused look of surprise.

"Does that number have a name?" I asked when she finished.

"Oh, right, sorry."

She grabbed my right cast and she wrote her name on it, as I giggled.

"One on each side, so you'll remember me wherever you look" she said, winking at me.

"Silvia" I read aloud.

"Yes, that's me" she smiled. "And you?"

"Rachel."

"Well, nice to meet you, Rachel."

"My pleasure, Silvia."

If I had been happy the day before, no words could describe what I felt that day every time I thought of Silvia.

The first week went by very quickly, we basically repeated the same scenes every day, I would come in, she would tie the laces of my sneakers, wash my hair, give me a massage, ask me to close my eyes and I still couldn't, we would talk until her employees arrived and only then, I would leave.

I was tempted to dial her number on countless occasions, not to get her to help me, but to ask her to come under that pretext, so I could see her for a few more minutes. The one hour she would spend with me in the mornings no longer seemed enough, in fact I think it never had on any other day, I always wished for more.

That day I followed my routine just like the last seven, only it wasn't going to end like the others and I didn't know it yet. After washing my head and giving me sensations that I liked more and more every day, she made me sit on the chair to dry my hair and do my ponytail.

"You have a beautiful mane, Rachel, when you'll feel better, I'd love to see you one day with your hair down."

Not that I couldn't wear it down at the time, but I always used to tuck my hair behind my ears to keep it out of my face, and now I was hurting myself with the gesture, so I'd better wear it in a ponytail.

"Sure" I replied shyly.

She smiled at me and when she had my ponytail perfectly finished, she stroked the back of my neck with her fingers as if she was combing the stray hairs underneath. As soon as she did that, I felt a shiver run down my spine and, without realizing it, I threw my head back slightly to seek more contact. I wished she would never stop, and Silvia didn't draw her fingers back. She continued with those caresses as we stared at each other through the mirror, and she began to brush the sides of my neck with her fingertips with a slowness that made me desperate.

Her fingers slid up my neck, causing me to shiver as she went on. When she reached my ears, she gently stroked my earlobes with her thumbs and then moved down again. She didn't stop until she came up against the collar of my shirt and began to trace the whole circle on my skin with her nails, while my breath became heavier and heavier, just like hers.

Little by little Silvia was sending me signals and I think she was touching me carefully so as not to scare me. What she didn't know was that, besides loving the patience and dedication she had with me, I also wanted to touch her, but I just couldn't.

I literally stopped breathing when her index finger slipped inside my shirt and followed the line of my collarbone very slowly, then the door opened and one of her employees interrupted that moment that was driving me crazy.

"Let me take you out for a meal, Rachel" she said just before she opened the door for me.

"You mean eating in a restaurant or something like that?" I asked stupidly.

No wonder she started laughing, what an absurd question.

"Something like that, yes."

"I don't know, Silvia, I just..."

"Come on, Rachel, I want to make sure you eat well for once, look at you, you're getting thinner every day, who knows what you're feeding on?"

I couldn't help but laugh again, and I wanted more than anything to accept her invitation, but the idea of going in those clothes and without a bra made me very uncomfortable.

"What's the matter, Rachel? Come on, girl, it'll do you good to get out and clear your head, you can't spend a whole month locked up in your house"

"It's not that, Silvia"

"Then what is it?"

"Look at me" I said, pulling my arms away from my body.

"Believe me when I tell you that I can't wait for you to walk through that door every day to do it" she said without holding back.

My heart stopped and I remained speechless, not knowing what to say, I looked at her terrified for a moment and then she took care of breaking the uncomfortable silence that I had created with my shyness.

"I'm looking at you, Rachel, what's wrong? What am I supposed to see? Tell me" She asked amused.

"Dammit, I can't go in these clothes, Silvia" I complained. " I'm not even wearing a bra and you don't know

how uncomfortable it is to walk down the street like this."

"I can help you get dressed, I gave you my number for a reason."

"Yeah."

"Yeah? But you're embarrassed, aren't you?"

"A little."

"I have the same as you, and you're not the first woman whose tits I see, Rachel, please don't be childish."

The truth was that she was right and, besides, I was sure that sooner or later she would end up seeing them, and not exactly because I was putting on clothes.

"Okay, I live on the second doorway, 3rd A."

"All right, I'll come by around noon. Is that okay?"

"Okay, hey, where are we going? Because cutlery and I haven't been getting along so well lately."

That got a laugh out of her, which infected me too.

"Don't worry, I was thinking of taking you to a pizza place I know, all you need to do is hold the slice and take bites, and if you get tired I can help you too."

"Fine." I replied, relieved.

I spent the rest of the morning on edge, not only because of the date I had with her, because I think it was a date, but because at noon she was literally coming to see my tits and just thinking about that scene made my legs shake. Me and her in my room. Me naked from the waist up, her watching. What if a finger of hers unintentionally brushed against me, or worse, what if she brushed against me on purpose? I felt the wetness between my thighs every time that image came to my mind. I took another shower and read while I waited. At noon she rang the doorbell.

I didn't bother to ask who it was, I just picked up the door phone and pressed the button with my elbow. I waited at the door while I heard the lift rise, and the closer I got, the louder and faster my heart beat.

"Hi."

"Hi, please, come in."

I invited her to walk ahead of me until we reached the dining room.

"You have a very nice flat, Rachel" she said, looking around.

"Thank you."

I felt more and more nervous, she looked incredibly beautiful, she had tied her hair back and was wearing ripped jeans and a tight plaid shirt that perfectly showed the volume of her breasts.

"I'm sorry about the mess, I can't take care of certain things, lately I feel a bit like Edward Scissorhands."

"Don't worry" she said, smiling.

The truth is that I was starting to feel uncomfortable with what I knew was about to happen, so I thought that the sooner we got this situation over with, the better.

"Will you help me and then we'll go?"

"Sure."

She put down her bag and followed me into the bedroom, I had already left the bra and t-shirt I wanted to wear on the bed. I stopped and she stood right behind me, I remained at the foot of the bed in silence, staring at my clothes and again I felt nervous.

"Do you want to stay on your back to make it less rough for you?" she whispered very close to my body.

I nodded like a little girl and her hands grabbed the bottom of my shirt and started to pull it up. I raised my arms and couldn't help moaning from pain, the truth is that certain movements caused such painful twinges that they took my breath away.

"That's it, shhh, that's it, Rachel, put your arms down" she whispered to calm me when she had finished removing my shirt.

I stood for a few moments with my arms at a ninety-degree angle, it was soothing. Silvia moved closer to me and held my arms in that position with her chin resting on my shoulder, not saying anything, just helping me to support the weight of the casts. She placed the palms of her hands just below mine and her fingers ran over mine with delicate caresses to avoid hurting me.

Suddenly all my fears were gone, I didn't care if I had no clothes on from the waist up as long as it was Silvia who flooded my back with her warmth. She pressed herself closer to me, I could feel her breasts through her shirt settling on my bare back and her hands leaving mine to wrap around my belly as she kissed my shoulder very softly. I thought I was about to melt when her increasingly wet kisses traced an intense path up my neck and her teeth nibbled my right earlobe, sending a huge shiver down my spine.

"I won't go on if you don't want me to" she said, nuzzling my ear with her nose.

But damn, I did want to. I wanted her to hold me tighter and make me hers, but what right did I have to ask her anything if I couldn't even touch her. I had never been with a woman before and the only thing I could think of doing to her was oral sex, but I was afraid, not because I didn't want to, I was afraid of doing it wrong. Not having my hands meant not having a foothold, not being able to grope her genitals or part her lips as I would have liked to. I couldn't see how I could please her in those awkward conditions.

"I can't even touch you, Silvia" I answered nervously.

Then her hands went all the way to my breasts and she covered them with her hands, massaging them with an overwhelming intensity that made me moan. I dropped my head back against her shoulder and she began to kiss my neck and ear gently.

"I don't want you to do anything, I've been wanting this all week, Rachel, let me please you."

"But it's not fair."

"Of course it is. You've never been with a woman before, have you?"

"No."

"Well, there are many ways I can feel pleasure without you touching me, so if you're worried about that, don't worry, I'll figure it out, I just want to see you now" she whispered.

That said, she spun me around and stared at my breasts for a few moments before she started kissing me. I rested my casts on her neck and Silvia shivered from cold.

"I'm sorry" I smiled into her mouth.

She devoured me more hungrily and started to pull down my trousers, I was so aroused that I can't remember the moment when my panties fell to the floor and I felt totally exposed in front of Silvia's gaze.

"Get undressed" I asked.

And she did, slowly removing every last piece of clothing that covered her body as I stared intensely at her and brought a trembling, aching index finger to caress the scar left by her appendix. She smiled at me and helped me lie down on the bed, propped herself up on her elbows and began to lick and circle my nipples with her tongue as I stirred restlessly with desire and pleasure. Suddenly I felt his hand move quickly over my belly towards my genitals and all I was able to do was spread my legs further apart to let her in with no barriers.

21

She smiled and began to massage me while I kissed her eagerly, clutching her face between my casts hoping not to squeeze too hard and hurt her.

I moaned intensely when I felt her fingers inside me, although it hurt a little, I really liked the rhythm with which she started to move.

"Does it hurt?" she asked in alarm.

"No. Please go on" I gasped.

And she kept going, until the little pain I felt disappeared and everything became real pleasure. I started to move my hips anxiously and she accelerated the rhythm until I came. And suddenly I saw the light, I knew how I could reward her and I couldn't wait for it.

"Stand here" I said pointing to my face.

She looked at me with astonishment and smiled.

"It's not necessary, Rachel, really, there's no need, when you're feeling better."

"Please, I want to."

Her eyes lit up with desire and she straddled my face leaving her genitals fully exposed just two centimeters from my mouth. I could see her terrific wetness and as I smelled the sweet scent she gave off I couldn't stop my naughty tongue from making her scream with pleasure. She grabbed the headboard with one hand and with the other she held my head to pull me towards her as she tangled her fingers in my hair. I clung to her thighs as best I could until I found the position that allowed me to lick her genitals more comfortably. I flicked my tongue in and savored every nook and cranny of her intimacy before I licked her clit as she moved gently against my mouth. She began to gasp, and with each gasp my tongue pressed against her pleasure zone and then slurped and massaged it incessantly. The gasps turned into intense moans before Silvia chummed on my chin.

She didn't take me out to eat that day, we ordered pizzas and ate in my flat without getting out of bed until the next day.

In the morning she helped me take a shower and we went down to the hairdresser's together to have my head washed.

"Come on, Rachel, close your eyes" she asked, running her hand over my face to help me.

I closed them, and for the first time in my life I didn't feel the need to open them. I relaxed and let myself be carried away by her caresses, I enjoyed Silvia's massage as I had never done before, nor would any of her clients, because it ended differently for me.

"Don't move and don't open your eyes" she ordered, tapping my forehead with a finger when she finished.

I obeyed with a smile and heard her round the chair until I felt her straddle me.

"Don't open them" she said again in an amused tone.

"No" I smiled.

"That's how I like it."

I felt her breath on my mouth and the tone of her voice became husky, her still wet hands caressed my cheeks softly and suddenly I felt her lips on mine in a deep, intense kiss. Her tongue forced its way between my lips until it made me die of pleasure when it came into contact with mine. My heart was pounding, my breathing had quickened so much that her breasts resting on mine weighed me down. I felt one of her hands find its way between us and settle between my legs as an amused and pleasurable tickle flooded my genitals at the touch, causing my hips to seek her hand in dismay.

Just then I realized that breaking both my arms hadn't been shitty luck, it had been the best thing that had ever happened to me.

We may have only known each other for a week, but with Silvia, I knew what it felt like when someone cares about you. She made me feel that I mattered, that I deserved to be loved, and above all she gave me the chance to know what it was like to love someone.

My Girlfriend Seeks a Boyfriend

"I don't understand you, Patri. Can't you see she's just using you? As soon as she finds someone she likes better, she'll forget about you, and you know that."

Kevin repeated those exact words whenever we saw each other, which nowadays was very often. He was my best and only friend, and we also worked together.

He was referring to Shannon, my girlfriend, or my friend with benefits, or lover. Or, as Kevin said, the woman who used me. What Kevin didn't know is that the story was much worse than what I have told him. In fact, I didn't tell him even half of it because he would be angry and disappointed if he knew the things I was allowing that woman to do to me. I met her three years ago at a bar, she was with her group of friends, and I was with mine. It turned out that we had a friend in common and that night we were introduced. We immediately connected, and between us, a special friendship arose. We became very close, we told each other everything and became inseparable. Whenever we had some free time, we would meet up, and you could always find us together.

In fact, we liked being together so much that the rest of our friends even bothered us; we couldn't wait to be alone again and, in the end, we always found some excuse to leave the group. Every time we spend less time with them, our circle was her and me. So much so that one of her friends once suggested that our behavior wasn't normal, that if we were together, we should say it openly, that it was fine.

That gave me a lot to think about, and I guess Shannon too. I knew that kind of friendship was not very logical; besides, I had never felt attracted to a woman before, I had always been with men, and so had she. Even so, I was aware that the desire I always had to be with her meant something else.

I loved things that I had never noticed before with anyone, minor details. I liked Shannon's sense of humor, how she lowered the sun visor to look herself in the mirror every time she got into the car. Even how she stirred the coffee after pouring only half an envelope of sugar. I loved the warmth of her body when she was near me, and I adored her touching me when we were fighting each other to pay for the drinks. Almost without realizing it and in the most innocent way, I had fallen in love with Shannon, with a woman. I loved her and silently desired her, and I was almost sure she loved me back, but I didn't dare say anything to her. What if I was wrong? What if it was just me who felt that way? I swear that I would have died to kiss her lips on countless occasions, but I managed to hold back.

Week after week, we hung out practically every day, until one day, while sitting on a bench by a lake, she started a conversation that led to the beginning of our story.

"Do you think our friendship is normal, Patri?"

I knew just what she meant, but my insecurity didn't allow me to jump into the conversation, so I left the ball in her court.

"What do you mean by normal?"

"Well, I don't know, we're always together, every day. We stay up until very late, even if we have to get up early the following day. I don't do that with any of my friends, only with you. I feel like being with you all the time, Patri. I can't wait to finish work to meet up, and as soon as we say goodbye, I miss you."

I was speechless, the truth is that Shannon was a straightforward person, but I guess I never thought she would be able to recognize all that.

"Shit, Patri, tell me what you fucking think."

"It also happens to me, Shannon," I smiled shyly. "I can't wait to be with you. I love being with you."

She looked at me confused, expressing with her eyes that she was as lost as I was.

"But I like men, and so do you. We are not lesbians, Patri." She said with overwhelming certainty.

"No, of course, we are not."

And the truth is that I really believed it. I thought that it was something that only happened to me with Shannon. I was sure that I would still feel attracted to men and never to a woman again if this ever ended.

"And what should we do?" She asked, worried.

"I don't know, Shannon. I'm as lost as you are."

The conversation stopped there, we didn't talk about it again until after a week, when we were in a disco dancing, and we almost ended up kissing in the middle of the dance floor. We both stopped in our tracks. For a few seconds, we exchanged a look of confusion as if surprised by the reaction of our bodies. Shannon reacted first, grabbed my arm, and pulled me to a quieter place where we could talk. The alcohol had disinhibited us a bit, allowing us to approach the subject from another perspective.

"Shit, Patri, we have to do something. This can't go on like this," she barked.

27

"Maybe we are lesbians, Shannon."

"Bullshit, I'm not a lesbian. Maybe you are!"

"Okay, you're not, but you fucking like me, and I like you."

"And what are we going to do?"

"We could give it a try; maybe it'll be good for us."

"Do you want to make out? Are you crazy? What would people think if they saw us?"

The truth is that the idea terrified me as much as it did her. How would I explain to my family that suddenly, at twenty-four years old, I liked a woman? Or to all the people who knew me? They would be shocked.

"I have at least suggested something, Shannon. You just ask and say no to everything. If you don't like my proposal, tell me what you want, and that's it. If not, don't ask me anymore," I answered grumpily.

"What if we go to that bar down the street where lesbians meet and ask someone?"

I burst out laughing.

"What exactly do you want to ask?"

"I don't know. We can ask if what's happening to us is normal, or how can we know if we're lesbians, I'm sure there's a way to find out."

"So you are starting to admit it?"

"No, I'm not admitting it. I know I'm not, but maybe there's something wrong with you. Something lesbian, fuck, I don't even know what I'm saying," Shannon said, also laughing.

"Okay, let's go, but I'm not asking the questions."

She smiled, and we went to the bar. It was only for girls and, the truth is that it was a little strange just to get inside, mainly because it was tiny. We immediately noticed how many eyes were glued on us. We leaned against the back of the bar, in a corner, as if wanting to protect ourselves from all those girls. We ordered some beers and watched them in silence for a long time as if the answer to our doubts would suddenly appear just by being there.

There was a bit of everything; girls who were just talking, girls who were dancing happily on the small dance floor, and others who were making out. This fact made me feel a bit uncomfortable, not because of what they were doing, but because that was what I had wanted to do with Shannon. I liked that practically since I met her, but I was afraid of her reaction. Those girls made me tremendously jealous because they did what they wanted without fear. Without hiding, they expressed their tastes openly, not caring who was next to them.

"What do you think?" She asked me.

I shrugged and took a long sip of beer with a blank stare.

"Fuck Patri, tell me what's on your mind, come on," she said, caressing my arm with affection.

I looked at her with a sad face. I didn't want her to feel sorry for me, I just felt that way, and I decided to pull a little of the rope that linked me to Shannon.

"I think I wish we could kiss as they do. I do want to try it, Shannon. No one has to know if you don't want to; it could be our secret."

It was there when we kissed for the first time. Shannon jumped on me and kissed me slowly for a few seconds in which I felt that I was touching the sky with my fingertips. I felt the warmth and softness of her lips as a shy tongue lightly brushed mine making my legs tremble. Then she broke away and looked in all directions to make sure none of the girls there knew us.

"Okay," She said.

"Okay, what?"

"Let's try, but in secret, Patri, you can't tell anyone, okay?"

"Okay."

That night we ended up in her apartment. We slept together, kissing and caressing, but without having sex. We were both completely lost, confused, and terrified of the new path we were taking, and we decided that for that night, we had had enough. I had never felt so great as the following day when warm, soft, and swollen lips woke me up with a shy kiss on my forehead. I felt her body heat flood me and a new kiss on my nose confirmed that I was not dreaming. I smiled slightly, and her lips rested on mine for an instant that filled me with life. I opened my eyes slowly and saw Shannon curled up in front of me. She was looking at me and stroking my head slowly, without saying anything, as if the simple fact of having me there was enough for her. I think that from that night on, I could divide my story with Shannon into five stages.

Stage 1

The first stage was the one of happiness. As in all stories, I guess this was the best and most beautiful, although it only lasted for about six months.

We started to enjoy our relationship in secret, allowing us to love each other without control. We stopped seeing each other on the streets and used both our apartments to let the desire we felt for each other run free. It was just three days after that night when we made love for the first time. We were carried away by what our bodies asked for, and the result was most satisfactory. Little by little, we experimented and improved our sexual encounters, making them a daily habit.

A couple of months later, she moved with me. We lived as a couple, but we were just two good friends for the rest of the people. Nobody ever found out that we lived together. We never invited anyone to our apartment, the only space where we could really be ourselves and show all we felt without hiding. During that time, it was enough with what we had, but our love was growing, and it was challenging not to show our feelings in public. Suddenly, it killed me not to be able to kiss Shannon whenever I felt like it. We had fits of desire that ended up in kisses at home, but outside I had to control, which began to affect me. It made me feel frustrated for depriving myself of something that straight couples could enjoy without any fear of being singled out.

One Sunday afternoon, one of those that we used to spend on the couch covered with a blanket and watching movies, I told her. I think that triggered the rest of the stages of our relationship. As soon as I became aware of everything that was beginning to happen, I regretted doing so. If I had kept quiet, maybe we would have been like at the beginning of our relationship. Now, I know it wasn't like that, that it would have happened sooner or later. Now I'm glad it was sooner rather than later because I lived a lie during those six months. Or a dream if you think it sounds better, but it was something that wasn't going to last. I guess the sooner I opened my eyes, the better.

"Shannon, I want more. I need more."

"More of what? What do you mean?" she asked, alarmed.

"I'm not saying I want to eat you out in the middle of the street, but it really pisses me off that I can't hold your hand or kiss you whenever I feel like it. I'm sick of lying to everyone, Shannon."

"Are you saying you want us to go out openly?"

"Well, why not? We've been together for six months now. I don't think it's just something temporary, we both love each other, and we're doing well. At least we could consider it."

Her face changed entirely, and she looked at me angrily.

"We already talked about this, Patri, and we agreed that we wouldn't make it public. I don't want to admit something I'm not; you know that I only love you, but we both know that this won't last forever."

Maybe she knew it wouldn't last forever, but I indeed hadn't even considered it. At least not seeing how good we were and how much we loved each other. I think that day, a tiny part of me realized that Shannon seemed to have plans in which I didn't fit, but I didn't want to listen. For the first time, her words killed me, and that was the beginning of the second stage, that of half-hearted happiness.

Stage 2

From that day on, I never mention it again for fear that she would leave me. We continued as nothing happened for six more months, and although I was still happy, it was not as much as initially. Something inside didn't allow me to feel complete happiness; my instinct told me that Shannon's words would not fall on deaf ears. I was sure that she knew that sooner or later, her feelings for me would come to an end, she would recover her life, and nobody would ever know about our secret.

We started to have arguments. At first, they were typical of any couple, but they were different as the months passed by. Shannon was always on the defensive, as if she was constantly pissed off because we had been together a bit more than a year, and she still loved me. I guess her plan wasn't working out the way she wanted to. One afternoon, while we were waiting in line at the cinema, we met a cousin of hers. She introduced me as her friend, something that killed me because, at the same time, it made me slowly lose hope of ever being introduced as what I really was: her girlfriend.

The three of us sat down to have a drink while the cousins caught up, and after a long time of conversation, her cousin asked a question that broke something between us.

"Is there any guy out there that you like, Shannon? You haven't been with anyone for a while, have you?

"I guess I've become more selective," she answered evasively.

After that, she changed the subject immediately. When her cousin left, she told me that she didn't feel like going to the movies anymore; she'd instead go home. The truth is that I didn't want to go either, I was hurt by her answer, and when we got home, we had a huge fight because of that.

"What the fuck did you want me to tell her? That I'm with you? That I don't have a boyfriend because I have a girlfriend?" She shouted at me.

"And why not? You could admit it and let yourself be happy. Nobody is going to kill us for it. It is only in your head, Shannon," I yelled too.

"Let me make one thing clear, Patri. I will never admit that I am with you or with any other fucking girl. We have this, and if you don't like it, you know what you have to do."

I had never cried as much as I did that afternoon. It was not only because of what Shannon had told me but also because I couldn't talk to anyone about it since no one knew about us. I had no one to ask for advice or a shoulder to cry on. I only had her. My group of friends had already dispersed, each one had gone their own way, and although I knew I could call any of them to meet up, I didn't trust any of them enough to tell them. I never had a best friend; I guess I only had acquaintances.

Stage 3

This was the stage where I realized that she would never admit it, that she was not willing to submit to what people might say about us if they found out. What we had was enough for her, but it was a problem for me. I think she would be willing to put an end to our relationship before even considering the option of coming out.

It was at that time when I met Kevin. He started working in the same department as me, and we immediately became friends. Just by chance, he was gay, one of those who openly acknowledged their condition. Every morning we had breakfast together. In the afternoon, when Shannon had Spanish classes, we used to meet quite often. I ended up telling him about ourselves. After all, he didn't know her, so it wasn't a betrayal. I think it was the first time I felt free, suddenly I was no longer alone, there was someone who understood me and to whom I could explain my problems.

I trusted him. I knew he would never betray me, I guess because he knew how hard it was to live a hidden love. The same thing happened to him too. I didn't beg him not to tell anybody for me; I did it for Shannon. Even though I didn't share her idea of hiding our relationship for a long time, I respected her. If she didn't want anyone to know about it, I would never tell.

"It seems very absurd to me that she doesn't want to recognize that she likes women. No one is with another person for so long just to experiment, Patri. From what you tell me, she loves you madly, maybe she is not a lesbian, but at least she is bisexual."

Maybe some time ago, Kevin's words would have relieved me or given me hope that Shannon would acknowledge our relationship. Still, at that point, I didn't care what my girlfriend was. She was never going to recognize it.

Suddenly, one day Shannon felt like going out. She said that we should go out again with our friends and widen our circle so we wouldn't end up as hermits. I knew Shannon was partly right; it had been a long time since we had met anyone. It was not a question of becoming antisocial, but I knew that, in reality, her motivation was different. I knew her too well. She intended with those outings to meet some guy and fall in love with him enough to forget about me. Just by her own, she didn't feel strong enough to leave me because she loved me too much, so I guess she went to a plan B, and I had no choice but to accept because, after all, it was just a suspicion of mine.

Stage 4

She got back in touch with her friends, and we started going out. At first, it was a couple of times a month, then every week and towards the end, every Friday and Saturday, as if she was desperate to meet someone to help her forget about me.

There wasn't a single time we went out, and she didn't start talking to some guy. She would flirt and dance with them while I stood there, dead jealous and outraged, putting up with her friends' comments and holding back the urge to cry. Each time this happened, we had a big fight, but she always told me that she hadn't done anything wrong and was just dancing with a friend. You may think I was stupid for putting up with that, and I guess I was, but I was so in love with her that I wasn't able to leave her. I think I gradually became a girl who accompanied her girlfriend to find a boyfriend.

What hurt me the most was that she was well aware of the damage she was doing to me, yet she didn't care. I don't know at what point she became so selfish, it was clear that Shannon didn't want to be with me, but since she was still in love and it was difficult for her to separate from me, she used me. It got to a point where she didn't mind hurting me while she was looking for someone to replace me so she could forget about our relationship.

It was perfect for her; Shannon was looking for a boyfriend, and in the meantime, she had me because when our anger cooled down, she treated me like a queen. She loved me; she showed it to me and made me feel great for two or three days until the weekend would come again, and the history would repeat itself. I never thought I would come to hate weekends so much, but at that time, I would get anxiety attacks as they approached.

"I love you, Patri," she said, crying during the last argument we had, "but this is not the life I have in mind. This is not how I see myself. I need normality."

Normality? I didn't even bother to answer her. I think I was slowly getting used to that; I knew that sooner or later, she would achieve her goal, and what surprised me the most was that now I also wished she would. I couldn't leave her either, so I wished a fucking guy would show up and get her out of my life. That's what I kept thinking over and over again, but deep down, I wasn't ready for it to happen.

Up to this point, my friend Kevin knew the whole story.

One afternoon, Shannon didn't come home at the usual time; she usually arrived around seven o'clock. If she was late, she would let me know. But this time she didn't, and after an hour of waiting, I worried and sent her a message asking where she was. I saw that Shannon had read it, but she didn't answer me; she didn't even bother. That day she arrived home almost at midnight and when I asked her why she told me that she had met a guy and went for a drink. She assured me that they had not done anything but that it just got a little late. She didn't have the delicacy to prepare me for it. She just blurted it out as if it was the most natural thing in the world. That was the beginning of the most painful stage of my life.

Stage 5

That night I didn't ask her anything else. I went to sleep in the other room. Initially, hoping that she would come to beg me to go to bed with her because I realized how much I would miss her if she disappeared from my life as soon as I lay alone in that cold bed. But she didn't, she didn't come looking for me, and I felt empty and used in equal parts. I thought about throwing her out of the house the next day. If everything was so clear for her, she should go to her fucking apartment and forget all about me.

I never understood that coldness with which she did everything. In the time we had been together, we had never slept a night apart. If I had been the cause of our discussion and she had left my bed, I would not have thought twice about begging her forgiveness, but she went to bed without remorse and didn't care that I was not at her side. That night I felt I lost a part of my heart that I could never recover again.

The following day I woke up very early. I had spent half the night crying with the certainty that she didn't tell me the truth and had gone further than just having a drink with that guy. The other half of the night I spent thinking about how I would tell her to leave the apartment. I replayed the words over and over in my mind, and for a long time, it was clear to me that I would be able to do it, but then I heard her get up, and I froze. My heart started pounding so hard I could hear it thudding in my chest. Anxiety and sadness consumed me again. Before I could react, she came up to me and hugged me from behind, begging for forgiveness. Crying, I pulled away from her and asked her to look me in the eye and tell me that she hadn't done anything with that guy, I knew she had lied to me, and that fucked me up even more.

At first, she insisted that she hadn't, but in the end, she ended up confessing that they had kissed. Shannon told me that she didn't feel anything for that guy, that she loved me, that she had made a mistake, and all those things usually said in those cases. I knew Shannon wasn't lying about that, that she had simply hooked up with him to try to prove to herself that she liked men, but apparently, she didn't get the result she was hoping for. I begged her to leave the house even though I knew she wouldn't, but I could not kick her out. My pain at the thought of her loss at that moment was sharper than the pain she was causing me.

That was one of the things I kept from Kevin, the first of them. I was sure this was only going to be the beginning. Shannon would insist on her trial and error method without giving a shit about how it affected me. Her cell phone was more active than ever. She wrote messages and received calls that she answered on the balcony. She always told me they were from work; I just hope she didn't think I believed her. One night she just didn't show up but had the nerve to do so the following day. The fight was terrible, and after shouting and crying disconsolately, she told me that it was better for each of us to part ways. Finally, something intelligent, you may think, but it wasn't like that.

She went to her apartment, but we missed each other so much that we kept on meeting. We kept on sleeping together and loving each other. I couldn't count the number of times she slept in my apartment, and I did in hers. It was worse than before, we felt the same, but we lived apart. I would never have imagined that you could miss someone in that way. The first nights without her, I could not sleep, everything seemed empty, and the smallest detail reminded me of Shannon. I cried every night, hugging a very different pillow from that warm and naked body that I liked to hug until I fell asleep.

She kept calling me to go out, and I was so stupid. I missed her so much that I preferred to have a bad time with her than none at all. After all, I knew well how it would end, with her fooling around and exchanging numbers with some guy and me playing the role of a spectator with one of her friends.

Maybe the logical thing for me would have been to start doing the same, to start meeting guys or girls to replace her, but I was not like that. I could not consider looking for someone else when I loved her, no matter how much of a motherfucker she was with me.

History always repeats itself. It seemed that the day would never come when Shannon would finally meet my savior. After all, that was what that man would be for me, the one who would free me from Shannon's charm and selfishness and the one who would allow me to mourn her for as long as I needed until I could rebuild my life. But that wasn't the case either. Finally, one day Shannon met a man she seemed to like, and they started dating. However, apparently, she didn't like him enough because she would come to my apartment when he wasn't around, and each time we would end up in bed. Now I was no longer her girlfriend. I was just her lover. If anyone had come to me with a story like mine, I would have told him that if he was crazy, to leave that woman at once, more or less what Kevin said to me when I finally told him.

"She's both a selfish and a bully, Patri, and you're stupid, dammit! She won't do it. That woman will never get out of your life. She needs you, and she knows it. The only one who doesn't know that is you. She'll never give you what you want or treat you the way you deserve. You have to be the one to put an end to this."

"Of course, it's easier said than done, Kevin."

I have to admit that, little by little, I became disenchanted with her. Her behavior no longer affected me as it did initially, and I no longer missed her as much. I guess the fact that we no longer lived together made me get used to having her less and less without knowing it. But I still loved her, that hadn't changed, maybe not in the same way as before, but without a doubt, I loved her.

"I'm not saying it's easy; I'm just saying that if you continue with her, she will destroy you. Just think about it. Now she has all she wants; a handsome guy to proudly walk down the street with and the woman she really loves to comfort her in bed. It's up to you, Patri. Do you really want that?"

"I think you're right; whatever I do, it hurts. I guess the most sensible thing is to distance myself from Shannon at once and start to get my life back on track without hiding."

I did not speak in vain. I did not say those words so Kevin would leave me alone. I was determined to definitively cut whatever I had with Shannon. As soon as I got home, I would call her to ask her when it would be a good time to meet to talk about it calmly. I didn't want to discuss it over the phone. I was closing the front door when she called to tell me that her boyfriend had a business dinner and wanted to go out for a while with me, that we should go out alone.

"Come on, Patri, so we can chat a little."

She didn't need to insist anymore; I accepted with pleasure, but this time not for her. For the first time, I did it for me because it was the perfect moment to break up with her. I didn't want to delay it any longer. After dinner, I got dressed up and went to the bar where we had arranged to meet. We greeted each other, and I asked to go to a quiet corner of the bar so we could talk.

"Shannon, I need to talk to you."

"Talk about what?"

"About us."

"Now? Fuck, Patri, can't we talk about it later, in your apartment?"

In my apartment? Fuck, how naive I was. She already had it all planned, her boyfriend was out, and she had the perfect excuse to spend the night with me.

"We're not going to my apartment, Shannon."

She didn't even listen to me because just at that moment, two guys stood next to us, and one of them asked Shannon something, so she started talking to him with a big smile on her face. I never thought her behavior would go to such extremes. I guess since her boyfriend wasn't enough to get rid of me, her plan was still on; she was still looking for someone to replace both of us.

I think it was one of the times it hurt the most. Whenever it happened before, I was with her friends, but that day we had gone alone, I had no one to even talk to, and she didn't seem to care about leaving me aside. She didn't even make an effort to try to get me into their conversation. She just ignored me.

After a while, one of the two guys left, and Shannon went to the dance floor with the other.

She didn't even look at me; she just left with him. I guess she took for granted that I would still be there when she finished fooling around with that guy, but that was too much. I decided it wasn't worth even bothering to tell her that I was leaving her for good. I would just never pick up her phone again, and in case she insisted, I would send her a message telling her to leave me alone.

I was heading for the door to leave when Maria came in.

"Hey, hi, Patri, it's been a long time," she said, greeting me with two effusive kisses on my cheeks, "Are you leaving already?"

Maria and I went to high school together, not that we were friends, but we took the same classes, and we got along pretty well.

"Aam, yes, the truth is that I was just leaving."

"Did you come alone?"

"No, well, my friend is over there, but I think she has a better plan, you know."

"Oh, well, I came alone, don't you think it's a coincidence?" She said with a smile.

I forced a smile at her with some effort, I think out of politeness.

"Let me buy you a drink, and we'll catch up. It's been many years since we've seen each other. You look great, by the way."

The truth is that I was a bit puzzled by Maria's behavior. I remembered her as a shy person, but it was clear that she had changed and had become a more daring and self-confident woman over the years. Suddenly, I felt like remembering the old times with her, so I accepted her invitation on the condition that it would not be in that bar. I didn't want Shannon to show up and fuck up our encounter.

That night I found Maria to be a very fun and spontaneous girl. She enjoyed things as they came up, without complications. She was one of those who lived the moment and took advantage of any opportunities. The truth is that I envied her. She was happily enjoying her bachelorhood, and I had been a bitter woman unable to meet anyone because I could not stop thinking about Shannon, the woman who used me as she pleased and had left me as soon as I stopped being useful to her that night.

Shannon called me that same night and also for several weeks. I never picked up the phone. I just left her a message saying that it was over, and another one a little later asking her to do me a favor and not call me anymore. In the end, she gave up.

After that night, Maria and I began to meet more often. Little by little, something was emerging between us, which led to a stable and sincere relationship. We have been together for almost a year and a half. A time in which I have learned to enjoy love without hiding. I walk with her hand in hand, and we kiss when we feel like it. My family already knows about it, and I think they were not even surprised when I told them.

It's funny because Shannon's insistence on finding someone to replace me led to me finding Maria. In the end, I was the one who found someone who deserved all my attention, someone who corresponds my affection and who loves me without secrets, without being ashamed of me. I think that was the problem with Shannon. In her mind, I was not enough for her.

I recently saw her on the street, I was walking holding Maria's hand, and she was with the man she was cheating on with me. She is now pregnant. I guess in the end she got what she wanted, what everyone expects from her, even if it cost her happiness, because I know she is not happy. I could see it in her face. She looks aged and dull. I'm not excited about that, but she was the one that chose it, and what still fucks me up is that she was willing to drag me down in the attempt.

From The Other Shore

Day 9 of lockdown.

Clare

"She waved at me".

"What? Who waved at you? What are you talking about?" asks my friend Isabel on the other end of the phone.

"That girl, the one on the other side of the river, she waved at me today".

"Really? Wow – she exclaims – this is the most interesting thing I've heard in days. How did it happen?".

"Well, I was walking Goku where I always do, on the riverbank, and she came out onto the terrace of her house, or balcony, I don't really know what to call it. We stared at each other, or so I think, because from 164 feet away, it was hard for me to tell where exactly she was looking, and after a few seconds, she raised her hand shyly" I smile nervously.

"And how do you know she was waving at you?"

"Good question. I also had some doubts, but then I remembered that we are in lockdown. I turned around and realized that I was the only person on the street at that moment and in that direction, so...".

"And what did you do? Did you wave back?"

"Yes, I raised my hand too. I think she even smiled at me when I did it".

"My God, Clare, you're not falling for a girl you can only see on the other side of the river, are you? You haven't even seen her up close".

"Don't talk bullshit. I haven't fallen for anyone. It's just that the situation is, I don't know, different".

"Yeah, very different, but remember, you don't know anything about her".

"I know when I go out to walk Goku she shows up on her terrace. I think she waits for me, and I like to wait for her to come out. What's wrong with that?".

"I guess nothing".

And suddenly Isabel starts laughing.

"What are you laughing about?" I ask, annoyed.

"Nothing, nothing, it's just that you've been living in that town for a year without knowing anyone, and it took a fucking worldwide pandemic for someone to finally wake up your fucking curiosity, and what's more, it's a girl who lives on the other side of the river. It couldn't be a neighbor of your block, who you could at least talk to through the window or the terrace. No, it has to be the one who is more than 164 feet away from you. Jesus, you are unique, Clare" she says, spreading her laughter to me.

"It's because I like challenges".

Shortly after, we hang up, and I decide to go up to the terrace to see if I can see her from there. I'll give you some background. I live in a small town, one of those where most of the houses are old. The Llobregat river runs through the middle dividing the town into two parts that communicate with each other by means of two bridges. I live in a block of apartments whose backside faces one of the two banks, the only one that is passable and where I can take my dog Goku out without going far from the block. On the other side of the river, there is a huge row of old houses, narrow, tall, three-story houses with a large plot of fenced land that dies into the river. In one of those houses is where I saw her for the first time the day before yesterday. I was sitting on a bench while Goku was sniffing everything before doing his business, and she went out onto the terrace, I guess to get some air because she just leaned with her arms on the railing and started looking from side to side.

The river, as it passes through this area, is very wide. I would say more than thirty meters. If we add to that that she has at least another twenty meters of land, I think we are about 164 feet away. At that distance, it is impossible for me to see her clearly. I can distinguish her figure that seems to me athletic, dark-haired, and of average height. I think she must be around thirty, like me.

Anyway, as I said, a couple of days ago we met for the first time. Since then, whenever I go out to walk Goku, I look for her on that terrace. I admit that at first, it was difficult for me to identify her house. They are all very similar and there are many, but in the end, I found a detail that helps me to distinguish it quickly. It is the only one that has a blue awning and whose land is tilled. It is not a patio, or a garden where I would have certainly put a huge pool. It is an orchard in which I swear there is nothing planted.

I go out onto my terrace where Goku is sprawled out basking in the sun and, for the first time, I look for her from here. That wave has tripled my curiosity for her. I identify her house right away, but at the usual distance that there is whenever I stand in front of it to walk my dog. I have to add that my block is very far to the right of her house, and when I say very far, I mean at least twenty meters. Even so, taking into account that we are now located diagonally, I would say that the distance that separates us is more or less the same as when I'm in front of it. I see it pretty well, three floors, the top two exactly the same, both with a window and a door onto the terrace with brown shutters. The paint on the walls looks a little chipped and cracked. Yes, I can make out quite a few details. I've always had good eyesight. I spend a long time observing everything. These days it never ceases to amaze me that despite the large number of houses with terraces I see, I hardly see people in them, even though we are confined, and sunlight is a luxury. Finally, and without seeing her, I decide to get back home and keep devouring chapters of the new series to which I'm hooked. This time it's Peaky Blinders, but at the rate I'm going in a couple of days I will have finished it, and I will have to find another one.

In the afternoon, after a little nap that I never take but that these days has become a vice, it's time to take Goku out again. Her wave from before has pleased me much more than I have recognized before my friend Isabel. Maybe it is because since lockdown has begun, I have been feeling more alone than usual or simply because I did not expect it, but I have felt a slight tingling in my stomach that has me a little bit worried.

We are already on the street. A few feet away, I see someone with their dog in the area where Goku and I always stand. I slow down my pace a little to give them time to leave. It is sad, but these days it is something very common. You are on the street with your dog, you see another person coming and you leave.

That's how things work now. As I walk, I can't help but look at her house, wondering if she'll come out, if she'll be watching me from the window without me being able to see her. What's her name? I'm sure she has a nice one. Finally, I get distracted. Goku is running after a pigeon while I pick up the gift he just left on the floor. I throw it in the trash and straight away, I hear a loud whistle that makes me turn around suddenly. My heart skips a beat when I see her back on her terrace. My pulse is racing, and I've just become very hot. What should I do? Should I wave at her? I don't need an answer. She has just waved at me. She has raised her hand again, now she is looking at me. I swear she is smiling. I squint my eyes to focus and yes, she is smiling. Automatically my hand has just raised and I'm waving at her with a goofy smile on my face. Goku comes back and snaps me out of my trance. I have to thank him for keeping me from waving like a fool who just fell in love.

Have I fallen in love? I hope not.

My new friend starts to make signs to me. She has something in her hand, but as she doesn't stop moving, I can't make out what it is. I make signs to her to stay still while I can hardly keep myself from laughing. What will the neighbors think if they see us? When she finally understands me, she extends her right arm holding something in her hand so that I can see it well. It's a cell phone. When I realize it, I smile again, and as soon as she sees that she first points to it with her other hand very slowly, second she points to me, then to herself and finally she puts the cell phone to her ear and alternates gestures between her and me. I understand right away. She is asking me if I want to talk to her on the phone and I nod yes insistently. Now you may wonder why we don't shout to talk to each other. It's quite simple. The river is always full of water. The noise it makes is enormous, not to mention that we are right in the middle of two waterfalls. You can hear a loud whistle or a scream, but to understand a word is impossible.

Okay, my friend and I agree that we want to talk on the phone, but how will we manage to exchange numbers if it is impossible for us to hear each other? In the distance, I see another neighbor coming with his dog. It's time to go. That's how things work, even if I don't like it. I try to make my new friend understand it through gestures, but it's impossible. Finally, I make signs with my hands to tell her to wait. She raises a fist. I would say with her thumb up, but I'm not sure.

As soon as we get back home, I rush to the terrace and look for her. I feel so happy to see that she is still there, only she is looking in the opposite direction to where I am. I scream like crazy to try to get her attention. I don't need her to understand me, just to hear me, but it's impossible. Although she seems to hear me, she can't find me, so I go to plan B. I go back inside and into the bathroom in search of the travel bag. I open it and take out a hand mirror. Yes, I intend to make signals to her just like in the movies, only I have no fucking idea how to do it.

When I come out, I feel a desolation that I don't understand. She's gone. I guess she must have got tired of waiting and gone home.

Day 10 of lockdown.

"How are things going with your mysterious friend? Have you seen her again? " asks Isabel as soon as I pick up the phone".

"Yes – I answer proudly – I saw her again yesterday afternoon, and she asked me if I wanted to talk to her on the phone".

"And how did she do that if you can't hear anything there no matter how hard you try?" she asks curiously.

"Through signs. It was a blast, Isabel. We understood each other by making signs like Indians. Now we just need to figure out a way to exchange numbers".

"You're both crazy, I'm telling you" she laughs.

"Maybe, but I'm dying to hear her voice" I sigh.

"Jesus, you say you're not, but you're falling for her. What if you see each other and you don't like her? Or worse, she's simply not a lesbian and she's only entertaining herself with you because you're the only one who pays attention to her. I'm sure the poor thing lives alone and is bored to death".

"You're a spoilsport".

"Maybe. I'm just saying be careful. I don't want you to get hurt".

"I know, but I think I'm going to take a chance".

"I didn't doubt it" she smiles.

And then we say goodbye. Goku claims his second walk. During the first one we haven't seen her, and I admit it has bothered me a lot, but there she is. For the first time I haven't had to wait for her to come out. As soon as we have set foot on the street, we have seen her, once again leaning on the terrace railing. She follows me with her eyes and a smile as I walk to our usual place, and once I'm sitting on the bench, she makes a sign to me and then raises a sheet of paper with a drawing that takes up the whole page. It looks like a letter or maybe a number. My eyesight isn't good enough, but even so I get excited, because I finally realize that it's a number. She's trying to tell me her phone number.

I stand up and get so close to the shore that I almost put my foot in the water, trying to gain ground so that I can read, but it's impossible. I don't know what number it is. A six? A zero? I'm sure it's a six because all telephone numbers start like that, but I don't want to risk it, so I give her clear signals that I don't understand. Then she smiles, tells me to wait and gets in. I focus on Goku. This time we've come down with the ball and I throw it several times to make him run and burn energy, taking advantage of the fact that no one else has come yet.

On one of those throws Goku finds a duck on the way and decides it's more fun to chase it until it flies back into the water than to look for the ball, so I turn around and find her looking at me with that smile that I'm getting more and more sure must be beautiful. How long has she been there?

Again, a signal. She asks me to watch, then she turns, picks up something and holds it up high. Oh my God! She has glued four sheets of paper and drawn the number on them. I can see it perfectly now. It's a six. I give a thumbs up as if to say "OK" while I feel the excitement run through me. Then she turns it over. Behind it is a three. My friend gives me another sign. This time she points in a direction behind me with her finger. When I turn around, a new furry one is coming to do his thing. Fuck, time to go.

I signal to her again like I did yesterday, but this time I point to my block and ask her to wait. She nods and Goku and I get lost behind the garage door. I go out onto the terrace again. This time she looks in the right direction, but my block is a double one. There must be at least fifty flats, so if I don't make signs to her it's going to be very difficult for her to find me. I take the mirror and look for the sun. I have no idea how to do it. I keep moving it around so much that I feel quite clumsy, but in one of those movements I see that I have managed to reflect the sun on the building in front of me. Finally! Now I know how to do it. Without losing sight of that point, I start to direct it towards her house. It takes me forever. Along the way there is a demolished building and that makes me lose the reference point, so I have to start again several times until I finally get it. I have the point reflected in her window and little by little I take it to her face causing her to make a very funny grimace.

Martha

Something blinds me for a second, maybe a flash of sunlight, but it's strange because right now it's behind me. It's blinding me again, dammit. I squint my eyes and start to look for the source of that blinding light when I start to see several flashes on a terrace of the block where the girl with the dog lives. An incredible feeling of joy floods me when I discover that it's her. She lives in one of the attics, no wonder I couldn't see her through the windows of the lower floors.

"Stop it, I've seen you!" I shout at her in amusement, even though I know she can't hear me.

What a noise this river makes. She's finally realized it. I have the impression that she's smiling and that makes me feel even more nervous. If I said I hadn't seen her before these days, I'd be lying. I've seen her walking her dog here on several occasions, not three times a day like now. I guess on normal days she would go to the dog park on the other side of the bridge and only take him out here when she was short of time. Anyway, something about her caught my attention the first day I saw her. I don't know if it was that carefree air or the fact that she always wears a tracksuit, something that really turns me on. I guess it must be both.

Since lockdown has begun, she always comes out here. I usually watch her from the window of my room. She usually doesn't stay long. It seems that among all the people who have dogs in this area there is some kind of silent pact. If someone comes, whoever is here leaves. I guess that way all the dogs have their time without their owners being at risk.

As I said, I usually watch her from the window, but there came a time when I started to feel like a stalker and at the same time a coward. It's clear that I'm attracted to this girl. I've always been a determined person and to put it simply, with a lot of guts, so why not let her know? I started to let myself be seen. Every time she appeared with her dog I went out onto the terrace. There's hardly anyone there, so when a person goes out it's difficult not to see them. She spotted me the first time and since then every other time she always looked for me nonchalantly. I know because before going out to see her I spied her first from the cover of my window. I know, that's cheating, but there are no written rules about this. And well, finally yesterday I decided it was time to take the plunge and try my luck. I waved at her, and a slight tingling sensation settled in my stomach when she waved back. And here we are, trying to get to talk on the phone.

From her terrace she starts to make signals to me. I see how she raises her cell phone and I smile. She wants the rest of the numbers, so I tell her to wait, and I go back inside to stick more sheets of paper with adhesive tape and write one by one all the numbers she is missing. When I go out, I see her leaning with her elbows on the ledge. It is one of those terraces that are part of the roof slope, so I can only see her above the waist, the rest of her body is covered by the roof.

I raise the next number and she seems to see it easily, although we must hurry because it starts to get dark and soon, we won't be able to see anything. When I raise the last number, she raises her arms in victory and so do I while I shout as if my team had won a match. The neighbors must think I'm crazy. With several gestures she tells me that she is going to call me.

Now I'm really nervous, but I can't let myself focus on that. My cell phone is already ringing and a number I don't know appears on the screen. I pick it up without hesitation.

"Hello, dog girl" I say in one breath.

"Hi, girl from the other shore".

Damn, what a sexy voice she has. A silence falls. For a few seconds I lose myself in the echo of her voice dancing in my head and she, well, I have no idea what she's thinking right now.

"Nervous? " I ask without taking my eyes off her.

"A little. Well, quite a lot – she admits – aren't you?"

"A little bit – I confess amused – what's your name?"

"Clare, and yours?"

"How nice. My name is Martha. Why did you call me?" I want to know.

"I don't know. Why did you give me your telephone number?" she answers cockily.

Well, well, it sounds like Clare is a warrior. Let's see how long it takes me to leave her speechless.

"Why do you think I gave it to you?"

"I don't know. My friend says that maybe you're bored to death and that's why you decided to try to talk to me".

Damn, I love that cocky tone.

"So, you've told your friend about me. I haven't told mine about you yet".

"But you will" she says confidently.

Okay, she's going to be a tough nut to crack. I like her.

"Do you really want to know why I gave it to you?" I insist.

"Yes".

"Easy, I like you. Now tell me why you decided to call me".

There, I left her speechless.

"I don't know – she hesitates – maybe because I like you too".

"Maybe? What a letdown, but well, I haven't used all my charms yet. You'll end up having a crush on me, you'll see" I say trying to sound confident.

"You seem to have it all figured out, don't you?"

"Pretty much, but well – I say at last – why don't we put aside this Alpha female stuff and talk a little bit?"

"Sounds good to me – she smiles – I know it's a very ordinary question these days, but how are you coping with lockdown?"

"Well, actually, I've only been home for a few days. I'm an ambulance driver and until four days ago I was on the street working, so I haven't had time to notice much about being locked up yet".

"And now you're not working? Your sector is overflowing".

"I might be corona positive. I had symptoms a few days ago and I was told to stay home. Yesterday I was tested and I'm waiting for the results".

"Don't fuck around! And how are you feeling? Do you need anything?" she asks worried.

"I'm fine. I was sick for a couple of days, the typical cold, but now I'm perfectly fine. I don't think I'll test positive. I just caught a cold at the worst possible time" I shrug.

"I hope you're right".

"I'm sure I am. And what about you? How are you doing?"

"Well, I've got Netflix worn-out, I've devoured all the books I had pending, and I kill my dead time sunbathing in the mornings. I've also downloaded a few recipes to see if I can cook something that doesn't taste burnt".

"Interesting. Maybe when this is over you can invite me in for dinner one day. I can be your guinea pig and try all those recipes".

"I'll think about it" she says, playing hard to get.

"Are you sure? I'm the most interesting companion".

"You already look like an interesting companion to me, even if from afar" she confesses.

Without ending our lively conversation, we both go into our houses. Night has fallen and it's cold, so I sit on the sofa, cover myself with a blanket and continue our chat while I peck at the leftovers from the noon meal. After a while we finally say goodnight and we agree that I will call her tomorrow, only when I look at the phone screen it hasn't been a while. Our conversation has lasted exactly two hours and twenty-six minutes. Time has flown by, so I send her a message to let her know.

"Yeah, I agree" she replies with a wink.

I go to sleep worried about how quickly time has passed by her side.

Day 11 of lockdown.
Clare

Today is a bright day. From early in the morning the sun shines brightly, and although we are at the beginning of April, it already invites you to lie under its sphere to receive doses of vitamin C, which is what I'm doing now.

I woke up very cheerful, so much so that while I was having breakfast, I came to the conclusion that more than cheerful, the word that defines my state is excited. Yesterday I was finally able to talk to Martha and I am eager to receive her call. At two o'clock in the morning I woke up and looked at my cell phone. I had received a couple of messages from her just ten minutes before. Isn't it a coincidence?

"We haven't introduced ourselves properly. This is me" she said, attaching a photo that left me speechless.

Martha is more or less as I had imagined her, only a little older than I thought. She is thirty-seven years old, although she looks younger. As for the physical aspect, I won't comment. I can't wait for this situation to end so that I can touch her and make sure she's real.

I also sent her a couple of pictures, and her response was two drooling faces, so I guess that she liked what she saw. We kept sending voice messages until I finally decided to call her again. I couldn't bear to see that she was recording the message and that I had to wait to hear her. I was anxious to know everything she wanted to tell me. I still do. During the call we began to enter the private sphere almost headfirst. In a few minutes I got to know her personal situation and she mine, in terms of relationships I mean, and from then on, and I'm not quite sure at what point, things began to heat up. The level of intimacy we had reached in just a few hours of telephone conversation encouraged us to go a step further, a step I had never taken before with any of my other partners. We had a conversation full of eroticism and sensuality and we ended up naked and moaning on the phone.

I can't help but get excited remembering all that happened last night, and even more so as I'm lying with only my bikini panties on under this sun that is getting hotter and hotter. I need to get those thoughts out of my head, so I grab my cell phone, open the browser (but not before making sure that Martha hasn't texted me) and start looking at the new books catalog. That helps me to calm down. I love books and I could spend hours reading the synopsis of the ones that catch my attention either because of their author, plot or even their cover.

While I am absorbed in my search, the screen changes and Martha's name appears on it, provoking an avalanche of pleasant sensations in me. All the anxiety I felt to hear her just disappeared, giving way to an immense feeling of happiness, a smile that I am unable to erase from my face and a tingling between my legs that forces me to catch my breath before answering.

"Hi, Martha".

"Hi" she answers with a sensuality that overwhelms me.

Did she do it on purpose?

"Can you talk or am I catching you at a bad time?" she asks while I try to calm down.

"No, I mean, yes, yes, I can talk" I answer, upset.

"What were you doing? If I may ask".

"Well, I'm on the terrace sunbathing while I'm looking for a new book to buy".

"Are you on the terrace? Me too. Get up and wave so I can see you, come on" she asks slyly.

"I can't" I answer, embarrassed.

"Why?"

"Because I'm in my panties. I never wear my top to sunbathe" I confess.

"Damn, now I'm even more eager to see you – she confesses mischievously – Do you know that it turns me on to sunbathe like this?"

Okay, now I'm completely turned on. How does she manage to get me all hot and bothered in one sentence?

"Oh yeah?"

"A lot – she says – come on, let me look at you".

"Okay, wait, I'll get my T-shirt".

"No, no T-shirt, I want to see you without it" she demands with a hoarse voice.

"Are you crazy? I remind you that half the town could see me".

"Come on, there's hardly anyone on the balconies. Besides, you go topless at the beach, and you don't mind, do you?"

"Yes, I do".

"Well, this is the same thing".

"It's not. Being seen by people I don't know is not the same as being seen by people I might meet at the bakery".

"Do it for me, come on – she begs – besides, I just got a call with my test results, and they were negative. We have to celebrate, right?"

"Oh my God! I'm so happy, Martha" I say sincerely.

And after those words and without a second thought, I stand up, and actually I think I do it because I'm craving it too. The situation turns me on, and I want more, and I'm sure that Martha knows how to give it to me. When I see her on her terrace all my nerve endings are aroused.

"Damn, you're gorgeous. Take a walk so that I can see you".

And I do it amused and excited at the same time.

"Gorgeous" she murmurs again.

"Come on, if you can't tell my nipples apart" I say as my sexual excitement rises out of control at the thought that anyone can see me through their window.

"I know exactly where your nipples are, I assure you, and when this shit is over, I'm going to lick them and shape them with my tongue as I please".

"Damn, Martha" I whisper as I sit on the lounger to try to calm my urge to violate lockdown rules and show up at her house.

"Don't hide, Clare. Let me keep seeing you" she begs.

"I can't, my legs are shaking, for real".

"Are you turned on?"

"Wildly".

"Well, in that case I'll have to take measures. Lie down and take off your panties" she demands while I obey, dying of desire.

Will it always be like this between us? I hope so. The intensity of her words is burning me inside.

For Daring

"You're not getting away this time, Olaya," my sister Jennifer says with a big smile.

I look at her and sigh, feeling defeated.

"Right, it's your sister's bachelorette party. This time, you can't refuse," her best friend points out as she answers a message on her cell phone.

"I didn't say no," I defend myself.

"You could show a little emotion or at least fake it," my sister complains.

"You know I hate bachelorette parties, Jenny. It's just a bunch of drunk women dressed up as who knows what, with dicks in their headbands, goofing off in the street only to end up drooling over a stripper. How exciting! As if the right to fuck with more men was the only thing you lose with marriage. You lose your space, your independence. Even your right to decide that you don't want kids without having to explain yourself or feel questioned or singled out as the selfish one who only thinks about her..." I say in a breathless outburst.

"Are you two at it again?" Jenny interrupts me.

I nod, and she sits on the couch next to me after her friend says goodbye to us and leaves.

"Is Alex still bugging you about having kids? I thought you two had already talked about it, and everything was clear," she says, worried.

"That's what I thought too, but he wants to be a father, Jenny. He says he is already thirty-eight, and he doesn't want

68

to have a child in his forties. I don't know what to do," I say, overwhelmed.

"What do you mean you don't know? You said you didn't want to have children yet, that you didn't feel ready. You are thirty-four years old, Olaya; you are still young. Having a child is not a decision that you should take lightly or under pressure. You shouldn't have kids until you are convinced that you really want them."

Sometimes, it seems unbelievable that Jenny is the younger of the two of us. We're not that far apart either, only sixteen months. But the fact that I've been married for five years and she's been jumping from flower to flower until she met David and finally settled down makes me seem so much older than her.

"Yeah, but Alex..." I whisper sadly.

"No buts, I understand his position perfectly, but that doesn't give him the right to put any pressure on you, Oli. Don't let him convince you if you don't see it clear," she insists.

"It's not that, Jenny," I start to get nervous and tap my fingers on the TV remote.

"So, what is it? Tell me, what is it, Olaya? Is there anything you didn't tell me?

I sigh and look at her in a daze.

"Olaya!" She yells is alarmed. "You're not pregnant by now, right?" she asks, shocked as I feel like I'm choking just to think about it.

"No, fuck no, that's not it," I reassure her.

"And what the fuck is it? Speak to me!" she asks in a bad mood.

"Alex is not insisting on having a kid, but he urges me to give him an answer."

"An answer to what?" She asks without understanding.

"He wants to know if I want to have children at some point, if I see myself as a mother."

Jenny doesn't say anything to me, just arches her eyebrows and grabs my hand, knowing I'm about to jump into the void and fall apart.

"I don't want to have children, Jenny," I confess, "neither now nor later. I don't see myself being a mother. I don't feel that instinct; I've never felt it. I can't give Alex what he wants."

"I understand," she says, looking at me wide-eyed and a little dazed, "you're afraid your marriage will go to shit, and when you tell him, you think he'll leave you."

"I'm not afraid, Jenny, and that's what worries me. Since I was aware of my decision and thought about the consequences it could have with Alex, I didn't care. Don't get me wrong, I love him, but we want different things, and the sooner we end this charade, the better for both of us."

"Are you telling me you're filing for a divorce?" she asks, alarmed.

"Yes, I do think it's for the best," I say with conviction.

At first, she looks at me with a disgruntled expression, but then she bursts out laughing and starts squirming while hitting her knees with the palms of her hands, as she does when she doesn't understand certain things.

"I can't believe it," she finally says, "mom and dad have been waiting for half their lives to get us both married, and now that I'm about to do it, you're splitting up," she mutters with laughter.

70

Everything is surreal and absurd, but I feel it's what I need to do.

"When are you going to tell Alex?"

"I'll wait until your wedding is over, it's your moment, and I don't want to take your limelight with my scandal." I laugh for not crying "besides, Alex is very excited about the wedding. He's really crazy about David's bachelor party. He's the organizer, so let's leave things as they are for now."

"Well, the wedding is still a month away. You have time to think, maybe you will change your mind, regarding the divorce, I mean. Maybe when you tell Alex he will accept it. He adores you above all things, Oli. By the way, you could follow his example and try to have a good time at the bachelorette party. I know you hate them, but I can't do it without my sister."

"I hate them all, Jenny, except this one. It's your party after all. I promise I'll change my mindset, and I'll be ready to enjoy it until the last minute," I say, kissing her cheek.

"I hope so, I don't want to see that sad face. It's only one day."

I smile, exhausted.

"One day? I wish it was just one day," I complain, "this Saturday is your bachelorette party, in two weeks Alex's company dinner. I can't say I'm not going because everyone goes with their partner and it would look bad if I don't go with him. And a week later your wedding. If I survive this month, it will be a miracle, sis."

"Well, if you look at it that way, and considering that you hate celebrations, you're right. After this month, there will be no one to stop you, Oli," she says with a smile.

Leaving my sister's house has taken a massive weight off my shoulders. Not only I needed to tell someone that I want to divorce my husband, but because she has supported me without judging me. Considering what is coming, knowing that I have her on my side gives me more strength and conviction to go ahead with my decision. I am very clear that my parents will not take it like Jenny, nor Alex's parents, whom I adore, by the way. This divorce will cost me much more than losing him. Many people around him with whom I get along very well will point an accusing finger at me, and therefore, they will cut me out of their lives. I count on all that. I have already assumed it.

I must admit that although I had no desire to come to my sister's bachelorette party, I started to have a good time from the moment I got on the minibus that picked us up. Because of the small age difference between my sister and me, we have always moved in the same circles and have the same friends. So, for me, the only strangers are a couple of Jenny's work colleagues, the rest I know them all, and I immediately let myself be wrapped by the good memories that bring the united group of friends. Before everyone went off to make their own lives, we had always had a great time, and tonight is not just a bachelorette party; It's like a reunion of old friends looking forward to having a good time.

The bus drops us off at a park near the restaurant. From that place to the door, my sister must undergo all sorts of tests. Ridiculous and embarrassing tests for her and terribly fun for us. I wasn't wrong about the little dicks. Jenny has been disguised as a sexy pirate, and the rest of us, the only thing we carry apart from a bandolier, is a whistle in the shape of a penis, disgusting but fun.

The dinner is the typical one; lots of laughs, lots of anecdotes, and of course, a stripper for dessert. I have nothing against that, but I don't like to be rubbed by a naked guy stroking his dick or his ass. I laugh watching the hard time my sister or the other attendants are having with the guy, who, I must say, is very handsome. The guy starts a tour around the table doing something to each of the girls. Before he gets to me, I make a gesture making it clear to him that he must pass me by. Laura, a friend from high school, is the only one who joins my cause.

"Seems like you are having a good time, sister, or is it just my impression?" Jenny asks with her cheeks on fire.

As soon as the girl next to me has gone to the bathroom, my sister sits with me to have a few drinks before leaving the restaurant.

"I'm having a great time Jenny. Maybe I'll sign up for more outings like this one," I joke, amused and obviously under that melancholic effect the first drink causes you.

"I don't think I believe you. You say it now because of the drinks," she says, clinking her glass against mine, "but tomorrow with the hangover, you won't think the same," she smiles.

"True, but what counts is the here and now, and I'm having a great time, Jenny. I'm glad I came," I say sincerely.

"And I'm glad you're enjoying it."

"Come on, girls, finish that. We're leaving," interrupts her co-worker and the party organizer.

"Where are we going?" asks Jenny expectantly.

"To a lesbian bar."

"Ummm, that's interesting," jokes my sister.

"A lesbian bar?" I ask in surprise.

"Yes, well it's a pub, it has a dance floor and tables if we want to chat. I've been there a couple of times, and it's charming. It's girls' night Olaya, we want to have a good time with each other, and we don't want to have guys fluttering around. So, we've decided to go to a lesbian bar; we'll have a few drinks and dance like crazy."

"There won't be guys trying to flirt with us, but there will be girls, right? Well, I don't know, I've never been to one, but come on..."

"We're a bachelorette party. It's obvious that we're partying and nothing else. I don't think they'll bother us, Oli," Jenny interrupts me, "and well, if they do, maybe more than one of them will like it."

The three of us laugh, looking at Laura, a friend we have always suspected of being a lesbian and who doesn't dare to come out. After dinner, many of the girls leave. Most of them already have small children who will demand their attention first thing in the morning and don't want to be dead with a hangover. So, in the end, only seven of the initial group go to that pub.

My sister's companion is right. The pub is just as she described it or even better. It is pretty crowded when we enter, and after ordering our drinks, we all hit the dance floor. Jenny was wrong in her prediction. The fact that we are a farewell doesn't stop some girls from approaching us. All of them are very nice, it's enough to say no, and that's it. It is a pity that some men do not understand the meaning of those two letters as quickly as women do. Some make jokes alluding to what we are missing, others leave, and some even join our party. We stay like this for quite a while, but my feet start to hurt, and I step back a bit. I need a break, so I lean against a column and just look around amused.

One girl catches my attention above all the others. Not that I'm interested in any of them, but this girl looks at me in a cheeky but subtle way. I don't know if I'm making myself clear. She doesn't look at me in a way that makes me uncomfortable or seems obsessive. She simply gives me glances to make me realize that I have caught her attention. The thing is that I can't stop looking at her either. Probably I do look like a stalker because the alcohol has made me bolder. The truth is, I don't hesitate a bit. I want to keep looking at her.

Although she looks like the badass on duty, she also transmits something else, I'm not sure what it is, but I like it. Suddenly, I feel a bit nervous, especially when I realize that I miss her glances when she is not looking at me. It bothers me that she isn't one hundred percent aware of me. I decide to go back to the group and start dancing again. I lie to myself, thinking that it's just to show that girl that I don't care about her, to show that I don't care about her attention. Still, I guess what I'm really trying to do is precisely the opposite. I want to grab her attention. I move to the rhythm of the music with the girls, and I sidelong glance at her slyly, or so I think.

"Do you like her?" asks my sister, who is already pretty wasted.

"What are you talking about?"

"About the girl at the bar, Oli, you keep looking at her," she says, leaning on me, placing her elbow on my shoulder with a somewhat dubious balance.

"It's not true," I defend myself.

"If you say so..." she turns around and keeps dancing.

Half an hour later, we get an empty table and decide to give our bodies a rest and keep the party with more tranquility. I choose a place that allows me to watch her. She hasn't moved from the bar. She has one arm resting on it and alternates her gaze between the whole pub and me until she gives me a smile and my nerves come to the surface again. I feel very flattered. I am delighted that a woman like her notices me, although I guess she is the typical girl that makes them crazy. She has said no to a few of them already.

"Why don't you go say hello to her?" insists my sister.

"Yes, Olaya, you should say something to her. She's undressing you with her eyes," says another of our friends.

"Cut the bullshit, please."

"If a girl like that looks at me that way, I'd get up and tell her to fuck me," Jenny blurts out, shaking her head.

"Jennifer!" I scold her laughing.

"Jennifer is right," seconds her best friend, who is drunker than she is, "I'd fuck her too."

Suddenly this has turned into a barrage of women talking about sleeping with other women. Between all that and the laughter we get from the comments, they're all throwing shots at me.

"You should go talk to her," says Nerea.

"I have nothing to talk to her about."

76

I pretend to be annoyed by their comments. Still, in reality, I am delighted to see that they have realized it's not my imagination. That girl is devouring me with her eyes.

"That's because you don't dare," Nerea insists.

"Yes, I dare. I just don't want to."

They are beginning to annoy me. I love challenges, and they all know it. They know that if they keep on teasing me, I'll end up giving in to show them that I'm not afraid, and that I'm able to do it. The worst thing you can say to me is that I don't dare, especially if I'm drinking a little more alcohol than I should, and in this case, I've got plenty of it.

"I think you're the ones who don't dare, you girls do a lot of talking, but I don't see any of you getting up."

"Because she's looking at you, Oli," laughs my sister, "I'll tell you what, if you go there and get a kiss from her, I'll relieve you of the burden of having to talk in church on my wedding day."

My eyes widen. I almost killed Jenny when she told me that the priest had asked her to choose two persons to read some passages from the Bible during the wedding. She picked his groom's cousin and me. Isn't it enough to be a witness? I'm not a shy person, but I am very discreet, and getting up there to read something in front of a hundred people makes me dizzy just thinking about it.

"And who's going to read it?"

"I'll ask mom; she's looking forward to it," my sister says with a shrug.

Now I feel like strangling her.

"And if she wants it so badly, why didn't you ask her in the first place?"

All the girls at the table look at us amused and expectantly, waiting for the conversation to heat up.

"Because you know how parsimonious she is about everything, Oli. Just to get up and walk down the aisle, she'll need five minutes, and I hate long masses. The sooner we get through to the banquet, the better. So, do we have a deal?" She asks, smiling.

"Done, but the kissing thing seems excessive and unnecessary. I'll go over and talk to her, nothing more."

"Come on, Oli, it's just a kiss," Laura says suddenly.

I feel like telling her to come with me and show me how to do it because it is clear that she is in her environment. It makes me angry that she doesn't tell us. We have been friends for as long as I can remember. She knows that we will not treat her in a different way because she likes women, but OK, she'll have her reasons.

"I'm married, just in case you don't remember," I say, showing my ring.

Jenny looks at me, arching her eyebrows. Now I feel like killing her. On a typical day, I know she would never encourage me to cheat on my husband, even if it's just a kiss for a simple bet. Still, knowing what she knows, she's not going to cease in her attempt.

"A tiny kiss, nothing more. Alex won't be mad about it; it's just a bet," laughs my lovely sister.

"All right, you can cross me off the list to read in the church," I say, pointing my finger at her.

I get up and go straight to the bar with a determined step. Just at that moment, the girl next to her leaves, and I stand next to her with a smile. Suddenly I run out of air and become tiny.

Now that we are so close to each other, I don't know what to say to her. All the self-confidence I had until a second ago has just disappeared. If I don't even know what to talk to her about, how the hell am I going to get her to kiss me? I don't recognize myself. It's clear that the alcohol is helping me because on a typical occasion, not only I wouldn't be doing this, I wouldn't have even allowed the conversation that has given rise to this.

The girl responds to my smile with what seems to be a forced smile. She has been looking at us all night, looking at me, and now that I approach her, she ignores me? Surely, I have just fattened her ego a ton and a half. Her looks were enough to attract me to her, I have bitten, and now she is no longer interested. Well, to make it clear, I'm not leaving here without my kiss.

"What did you bet?" she asks, surprising me.

"What?" I ask with the bit of air I have left and an enormous sense of guilt.

She looks at me smiling but not angry. She seems to be having fun with the situation and enjoying that she has caught me. She has discovered my cards and has the power to decide if I win the bet or not. I'm not good at lying, so I don't look for any excuses.

"How do you know I bet anything?"

"Ummm," She sighs and shrugs, "I've been watching you for a while."

"Yeah, I know you did."

"Did it bother you?" She asks with a half-smile. "Sorry, I didn't mean to bother you. From time to time, I come to this bar, and I stand here, on this side of the bar," she points out.

Suddenly I feel trapped by her words. Her badass look doesn't match at all with the way she talks. I disconnect from the music and the commotion and just focus on what she tells me. I really want to know why she was looking at us so much.

"I like observing people," she confesses, "I imagine what they do for a living or what their lives are like. I like guessing the reason that has brought them here, to see if they are having a good time, to find those who are discovering themselves and are scared to death..."

Her look between accusatory and amused draws a smile on me.

"Do you think we are discovering ourselves?" I ask, intrigued.

"No, it's clear that you're just on a bachelorette party. Just look at that little dick hanging around your neck," she points out with some disgust.

"Oh yes, I didn't even remember," I say with the same disgust as she does.

I take off my whistle and throw it on the ground.

"You don't have to throw it away," she smiles.

"Believe me if I tell you that I am as much disgusted as you, about the whistle itself, I mean."

"Yeah," she smiles with raised eyebrows.

"So, you just come here to people-watch? You don't come here to flirt?" I ask, full of curiosity.

The way she smiles changes and becomes more like her, a bit more mischievous and cockier, which both attracts me and makes me nervous.

"Don't be mistaken, I like to observe; to imagine things about people helps me to forget about my own. But I also like to fuck," she says, cutting my breath, "the truth is that I really like fucking," she affirms, focusing on me as I feel my legs tremble and an unknown excitement grows inside me.

I take a sip of her drink without even asking for permission and look towards our table, suffocated.

"You still haven't told me what you bet," she insists again.

"Nothing, it doesn't matter anymore, you've found out, so I've lost." I give up.

"But you came. I've been watching you for a while, as I said before, but I was mainly watching you; you've already noticed," she says, narrowing her eyes.

"And why were you looking at me?"

"I find you attractive," she says bluntly.

I don't know what to answer. I feel very flattered by her confession. I'm used to men liking me, and to suddenly have a woman like her telling me that she finds me attractive is very nice.

"So you lost your bet," she says thoughtfully, "that makes me rule out that what you've been asked to do is to come here and talk to me because you've already done that, and yet you say you lost."

She gets closer to me with a seductive air that sweeps me up. I'm lost.

"If you tell me, maybe I can help you win," she whispers, letting the tip of her nose brush against my ear.

I feel a pleasant shiver run through my body, I'm short of breath and speechless; thinking about the idea of kissing her now that I have her in front of me makes me feel that this will not be enough. I have gone from approaching to get a simple kiss to wanting her body to stick to mine and fill my mouth with her tongue.

"You look nervous. Are you OK?" she asks slyly.

No, I'm clearly not OK; this girl makes me feel things that only men had caused until now, which makes me uneasy and scares me.

"You're having fun, aren't you? That's your reason for being here? To find a difficult challenge?" I ask angrily, "I've seen you say no to a bunch of girls, even though you say you like to fuck so much. I'm sure you've already fucked half the girls in the bar, and you're now only interested in the new ones. You've watched me and provoked me until you got what you wanted; I came to you just to boost your ego. How does it work? You make me horny, fuck me in the bathroom, and then you disappear?"

She looks at me with wide eyes but an amused face. Maybe she didn't expect me to be so angry. However, I have the feeling that the fact that I have shown her a bit of my bad temper instead of scaring her has awakened her interest even more.

As soon as I finished talking, I ducked my head in shame for what I just said. I have unloaded against her all the anger for wanting to kiss her. That way of whispering in my ear has annoyed me very much. I don't know if she has done it to seduce me or as revenge for approaching her because of a bet. In any case, her gesture has excited me quite a lot, and that throws me off. I'm used to controlling situations, and this one catches me off guard.

"Wow," she says, arching her eyebrows, "you've got a lot of nerve girl, it's fascinating all that theory you've invented about me, especially the part about fucking you in the bathroom.

I really liked that part," she confesses smiling, "although I wouldn't fuck you there, it would be too obvious."

This time is me who arches the eyebrows. Is she serious?

"And, where would you fuck me, if I may ask?" I ask, agitated.

"There," she says with confidence, pointing to the corner of the bar.

I let out a stifled sigh mixed with a wry smile. That's what she notices. What she doesn't is the enormous desire I have for her to do what she just said and fuck me exactly where she pointed. I am so excited by her confidence and how she has brushed my arm with her fingers that it is almost unbelievable.

"There?" I repeat incredulously, "you'd fuck me there in front of everyone? I can tell you love to brag," I say defensively.

It seems that showing my anger is the only way I can hide how helpless she makes me feel.

"What's your name?" she asks, cutting me off.

"Olaya."

"Olaya," she repeats with pleasure, "that's a beautiful name, my name is Lara. What was the bet, Olaya? Please tell me," she begs.

He has me totally baffled. I know she's up to something, and what really pisses me off is that I am playing along.

"I had to get a kiss from you," I smile, regaining my composure and looking a little more confident.

"I wonder how the owner of that ring would feel about that?" she asks, pointing to my wedding ring.

"That's none of your business," I reply grumpily.

"Right," she admits, "What happens if you lose the bet?"

"I'll survive," I reply in disgust.

"Do you like to gamble?"

I sigh deeply and try to relax. Her calmness and confidence are entirely disarming me.

"Not that I like it, but if I get challenged, I accept. I don't want to lose," I say with a shrug.

"I'll let you win that bet on one condition," she says, getting even closer to me.

Without me being able to react, she places a hand on my waist and brushes her cheek to mine, making me burn.

"What condition?" I whisper, upset as she moves her hand up to my neck. She caresses my right ear with one finger and whispers in my left. My legs are trembling.

"I'll give you that kiss, but only if we go to that corner. Mind you, I kiss for real, with my tongue."

Her comment just sets my pulse racing, and I'm having a hard time thinking clearly.

"And that's it, that's the only condition, that we go to the corner?" I ask, trying to regain the calm she has stolen from me.

"Yes."

I smile, arching my eyebrows. I'm going to win the bet, and besides, she's going to kiss me well, the way I want right now.

"Don't smile Olaya, do you know what's going to happen after I kiss you?"

"No," I gasp, suddenly scared.

She grabs my hand and pulls me into the corner. I offer no resistance to the relentless Lara, who pushes aside a stool and presses me against the wall, leaving part of my body hidden by the corner of the bar and covered by hers. Our table is to the left; I look over to make sure they are watching as Lara continues with her body pressed against mine and I get more and more turned on. They all look at me with a smile and anticipation that indicates they know this whole situation is slipping through my fingers. My sister looks me straight in the eyes with a severe gesture and utters one word slowly so I can read her lips. "Do it," that's what I read, and I shudder because I know Jenny, and she isn't just referring to the kiss. I stop looking at them and focus on Lara, completely stunned.

"OK, Olaya, are you ready?" she asks, whispering.

I nod, and Lara tilts her head slightly as her mouth approaches mine. Her lips didn't even brush mine, and I can hardly breathe or think. My mind blurs as the tip of her tongue brushes my lips to make its way in. Without thinking and full of desire, I place my hand behind her head to draw her in, trapping her tongue between my lips, playing mine around hers. I can't think of anything else but to keep kissing her. Lara kisses fucking well, her tongue licks mine, her lips suck mine, her fingers get lost in my hair, and her body is completely glued to mine.

I separate my lips from hers just for a moment without detaching a single millimeter from her body; I need to breathe. Still, while I do it, she keeps giving me tiny kisses on my lips. She brushes my lips with the tip of her tongue and then kisses the area. She has me wholly hypnotized. Lara lets me breathe, but she gives me no respite to diminish my excitement. I feel entirely dazed and full of desire, clouded, unable to reason.

"You've already won the bet," she whispers into my mouth.

I nod without looking away from her lips, entirely at her mercy.

"Do you know what's going to happen now?" She asks with overwhelming sensuality.

I shake my head in her hands, and again she brings her lips to my ear to whisper.

"I'm going to make you cum right here," she says.

My reaction? I let out a stifled sigh and squeeze my legs tightly together to quell the prick of pleasure I felt in my sex as soon as I heard her.

"I will hardly touch you, Olaya," she continues whispering, "there is little light here, and no one will notice. The only ones who will know that you are cumming will be you and me. Because I assure you that you will cum."

Lara has just made me so horny that I wouldn't care if they saw us right now. I can't wait for her to keep her word and to fuck me.

"How do you plan to do that?" I manage to say with some effort.

"Like this."

She kisses me again, placing one hand on my back and the other on my ass. Just like that, and making as if we were sensually dancing, she starts rubbing her sex against mine. She makes slow movements so that the sensation of contact is full. I follow her, guided and blinded by my own pleasure. I don't own my hip movements or my body. I like it so much that I feel I reach a point where I can no longer continue kissing her.

She is right; if she continues like this, I will cum right here. Her caresses and the fact of being surrounded by so many people have excited me so much that I don't recognize myself. Still, there comes a moment when suddenly I don't want to continue. To my surprise, I realize that I need her to touch me. I want to feel her fingers between my legs, so I move away suddenly and take her by the hand to go to the bathroom.

For the few seconds of the journey to the bathroom, I feel petty and wonder what the fuck I'm doing. Still, Lara is glued to my back and walks so decisively, squeezing my hand that my consciousness fades, and I only listen to my body's desire. All the stalls are occupied when we enter, and my heart is about to burst out of my mouth.

"Shit," I moan under my breath.

Again, she holds me from behind and places her hands on my hips, pressing her pelvis against my ass.

"Can you hold on?" she whispers in amusement.

Before I can reply to that brazen display of Alpha female, a stall door opens, and we are next. I can't believe what I'm doing. I've never fucked in a public restroom; I've always been disgusted by that, and to make matters worse, this one isn't exactly clean. Still, I stick my back to the door and hike up my skirt, desperate for Lara to touch me. She looks at me for a moment before moving, with the skirt around my waist, offering my body to her. For an instant, I feel dirty. Still, it passes as soon as Lara comes closer and pulls down my panties with an expert hand. She gets closer to me, and her right hand rests on my sex, allowing me to feel all her heat. I throw my head back and sigh deeply as she begins to caress and kiss my neck. Her fingers move wisely and slide and glide smoothly all over my sex. Lara licks my neck, going up to my ear, kissing it, biting it before approaching my mouth to devour it for a moment. She looks at me and intensifies her caresses on my sex. I close my legs, catching her hand and stifling an intense moan. Lara grabs me with her free hand by the nape of my neck and puts her knee between my legs, forcing me to open a little to give her hand more freedom of movement again.

"You like this, don't you?" She asks while at least three of her fingers are placed on my clit.

I nod, and another intense moan comes from my throat as I press my sex against her hand. I am on the verge of cumming; pleasure has been devouring me for a while now. Her fingers trace circles, and every now and then, slide to the entrance of my pussy to gather my wetness before returning to my clit. I moan more intensely as she picks up the pace, and my hips begin to move rhythmically against her fingers.

"Are you going to cum, Olaya?" She whispers in my ear. Are you going to cum for me?"

Hearing her dirty talk so close to my ear only intensifies my excitement and pleasure.

"Yes..." I gasp. "I'm going to cum."

I don't manage to say anything else. I just cum in her hand while she looks at me, satisfied. I grab her shoulders with both hands to catch my breath, and as soon as I do, I pull up my panties and skirt as if nothing has happened, pushing Lara against the wall. She leans her shoulders in amusement and pulls her ass away from the wall offering it to me when she observes that I start to unbutton her pants.

"Are you going to fuck me, Olaya?" She asks, biting her lip.

I glare at her. I can't wait to do it, but I can't stand that arrogance.

"Yes, Lara, I'm going to fuck you," I say, full of confidence.

She gets serious, pulls down her pants to her ankles, and looks at me, burning with desire. I pull down her panties and place my hand on her sex in the same way she has done on mine. I feel very strange and excited simultaneously; it is the first time I touch a pussy different from mine, and I really like the feeling. I feel her warmth and softness. I run along her folds. I am filled with her wetness and feel fantastic when I realize that what I am doing pleases her.

Is it OK like this?" I ask, getting lost in her folds.

"Ahaa," she replies with a satisfied smile.

I use my other hand to caress her breasts. They are not very big, but they are also the first ones I touch that are not mine. I like it, too; feeling the delicacy of that part of her body makes me realize that fucking a woman is extremely satisfying.

"Get inside," she says suddenly.

I'm paralyzed. I don't know how I should do it, and she smiles, amused and excited at the same time.

"Stick a finger in my pussy," she gasps.

I obey. I put it in slowly and look at her, waiting for a reaction.

"Stroke it," she begs.

Now I understand what she needs, and I give it to her. I use that finger to caress her insides in the same way I do when I masturbate, gently but intensely. Although I find it a bit uncomfortable because of the position, I manage to use my other hand to touch her clitoris. At the same time, my finger gets lost inside Lara until she cums. I find it the most exquisite thing I have ever experienced while caressing another body.

When we leave the bathroom, we wash our hands, and we go straight to the bar. I'm both dying of thirst and wanting to drink alcohol to assimilate what I just did. I look over to the table as they serve us, three of the girls are gone, and Jenny looks at me with a broad smile as she stands up and walks over to me.

"It's time to go, Oli; the minibus will be at the door in ten minutes. Are you coming or staying?"

I hesitate for a moment, but for tonight I've done too many crazy things already.

"I'll be right there, Jenny."

She nods with a smile, waves to Lara, and turns back to the table.

"Are you leaving already?" Lara asks.

"Yes," I answer with a strange sense of desolation.

"Well, it was a pleasure to meet you, Olaya," she says without further ado.

That bothers me; it is like she doesn't give a shit about what has just happened.

"Don't you want to give me your number?"

I don't really know why I ask for it. I didn't have it in mind, but it just came out like that.

"I'd love to, Olaya, I really would," she answers very seriously, "but I'm not into being someone's side dish. I am not anyone's escape route and much less that of a married woman. Don't be offended. I loved fucking you, and if you were single, I assure you that I would ask you for a date to get to know you better. Still, it is not so, and our paths are separated here. I wish you the best, Olaya."

She kisses my lips and disappears into the crowd before I can say anything. No one asks me or says anything; they are all too drunk and tired, so as soon as we get into the minibus, they are almost asleep. All of them except me, who can't close my eyes without the image of Lara and me in the bathroom returning to my head and clouding my mind. Then I think about how she said goodbye to me, and I feel bad, leaving aside that I shouldn't have let this happen.

"Tell me everything!"

I almost had a heart attack. Jenny jumped on my bed, waking me up with that request that, for a moment, left me unsettled.

"Beat it, Jenny, don't you have a home?" I grumble moodily.

"I've been biting my nails for two long hours waiting for you to wake up, and I can't stand it anymore. It's almost four in the afternoon, Oli; get up now and tell me what happened in the bathroom," she demands.

I open my eyes and sit up, moving my head like a radar and my heart beating too fast.

"Relax, Alex has gone with David. They have a soccer match, don't you remember? No, of course, how can you remember if you were almost in a coma" she answers herself.

I drop back down and sigh in relief while Jenny looks at me with a huge smile and her face of expectation.

"What have I done?" I ask myself, covering my face with both hands.

"Don't hide, slut," she says, pushing my hands away, "that's what I want to know. What did you do?" she asks, amused.

I look at her, and I can't help a huge smile as soon as I think about what I did.

"Oh my God!" she exclaims, impressed, "did you fuck her, Oli?"

"Could you be a little less ordinary, Jenny?" I ask, trying to buy some time.

"Cut the crap, Oli, unless you fell in love with her and she fell in love with you, which I doubt, what you did yesterday is called fucking. Shit, I don't believe it," she says laughing "thank goodness it was only going to be a kiss," she continues roaring, "you're my idol, Oli, what's it like? Fucking a woman, I mean, they say it's amazing. Did she do it right?"

I nod insistently without wiping the smile from my lips; no matter how hard I try, I can't.

"Better than with a guy?" she asks, curious.

"Different."

"What the fuck kind of answer is that?" she whines.

"You've said it before, Jenny, we fucked, there was no foreplay or other attention, still..." I remain thoughtful "fuck, even so, I had an orgasm that left my legs shaking. It was as if she knew exactly what to do to kill me with pleasure. Everything is different, Jenny, even if it was a simple fuck in a bathroom, her touch was infinitely softer and wiser, everything is more sensual, or maybe it's because I was a little drunk, I don't know," I whisper with a lost look.

I spend the whole week feeling bad for not regretting what I did. I cheated on my husband, and I have cheated on him with a woman. Still, I don't feel guilty; the fact of having decided beforehand that my marriage should end, I guess, makes me feel free to do whatever I want, even if it has not yet ended. That's what makes me feel the worst, Alex is a good man, and I don't feel one bit of guilt for cheating on him. What kind of woman am I?

I plan to go back to that pub. I need to see Lara again, I can't get her out of my mind, and it's not just because of what we did. I really liked her personality. There was something that seduced me, and I want to get to know her a little better. Maybe she can help me dispel all the doubts I now have because of her.

But all that must wait. First, I must solve my personal issues with Alex; just because I don't feel bad for what I have done doesn't mean I don't respect him. This Friday is his company dinner, and I will go with him as promised. My crime and my needs will have to wait.

Alex arrived just twenty minutes ago and is already showered, groomed, and perfumed.

"Are you ready, sweetheart?" He asks as I take one last look in the mirror.

"Yes, it'll be just a second. May I know why you're so excited? It's just a dinner party, Alex."

"A dinner where we're celebrating something," he tells me happily.

"Oh yeah? What are you celebrating?"

"Remember that contract I told you about?" he whispers, hugging me from behind.

"Ummm, yes, the one you were disputing with another company, right?"

"Exactly, we met with the client again today, I made a mind-blowing presentation, and it's ours. We've already signed it."

For months, he has been talking to me about how important this project is for his company and for him, and he has finally achieved it.

"I'm thrilled, Alex," I say, sincerely kissing him again, "I knew you would get it. They put you in charge of the project for a reason."

"Well," he says proudly, "it wasn't just me; the truth is that I have a great team."

My husband places his hands on my hips to press me against him. I feel the hardness of his member on my sex. On the one hand, I get excited; on the other hand, I don't feel like doing it now. I just don't feel like it.

"Just a quickie," he whispers, caressing my breasts.

"Not now, Alex; I've spent an hour getting ready. Do you want us to be late?"

It's the first time in the seven years we've been together that I've made up an excuse, so he gives a hoarse sigh into my neck but nods in agreement and doesn't complain. By the time we get to the hotel, almost everyone is there.

"For God's sake, how many people work at your company, Alex?" I ask, alarmed.

This looks like a wedding banquet. It is full of round tables everywhere, generously covered with food and drinks. Almost everyone is standing around, greeting each other, huddling, and jumping from one person to another.

"I really don't know; we've hired a lot of people in the last few months," he answers, amused.

I stand next to him, all this overwhelms me and the only person I know is his secretary, and although I try, I can't see her, there are too many people. Alex greets his colleagues like a true leader; everyone comes to congratulate him and shake his hand. It seems that my husband has done a great job, and I feel proud of him. Alex introduces me to each of his colleagues. I just say hello and smile just enough to look polite, but not enough for them to start a conversation. It's not that I don't like them. I'm sure they're great people, but these situations overwhelm me, and I prefer to stay in the background.

"When are we going to sit down?" I ask tiredly, "the heels are killing me."

"Soon," he says like an automaton as he continues to greet one and all.

I understand his desire to continue. Everyone congratulates him; they shower him with the best compliments and give him one smile after another. So, of course, he doesn't want to sit down. After several more minutes in which I hold the type as best as I can, Alex says goodbye to an older man. It seems that we are finally going to set course to our table. I will be able to rest from these horrible heels, but everything goes wrong. My husband opens his arms excitedly to receive the girl who was behind us and says:

"Here is the woman who has helped me prepare the project and is as worthy of congratulations as I am."

After those words, he hugs the woman for a few seconds, and with a happy gesture, he undoes the hug and turns to me:

"Honey, this is Lara, the company's latest big signing and the best graphic designer you'd ever met."

After that, he moves away, and my legs begin to weaken when Lara stands before me with a big smile and, like a real actress, pretends not to know me and greets me with two effusive kisses on the cheeks that make me feel a suffocating and scorching heat. I don't know if it is because of the embarrassment of the situation or because her lips have brushed my skin again.

"It's a pleasure, Mrs. Ayala. Your husband is an incredible man; I'm delighted to be able to work in your team. If you'll excuse me, I have to say hello to a friend."

I don't even manage to answer her or smile back. Lara disappears in the crowd, and I'm paralyzed. Still, stunned, terrified, excited, pissed off, upset, sensitive, and blinded by the surprise of finding her here.

"Honey are you OK?" asks my husband, bringing me back to reality.

Reality hits me like a hurricane. After recomposing myself a bit, we go to our corresponding table, a round one with six chairs and two little signs indicating that two of them belong to us. For a good while, I manage to disconnect; my husband tells me everything that this new project implies while people gradually sit down in their seats, and I pretend to understand what he is saying, even if it is not so.

"How long has Lara been working with you?" I ask suddenly.

My husband gives me a skeptical look, and after dwarfing his eyes a little, he answers:

"Almost six months, Oli, I've told you about her many times, although perhaps I've always referred to Lara by her last name, Vazquez."

"Oh, yes," I hasten to say, "I just didn't imagine her so beautiful," I murmur after a betrayal of my subconscious.

"You don't have to worry, Oli," she says smiling, "I love you, and Lara is openly lesbian. You can be twice as calm."

I should be calm, but now I'm tachycardic. I think this is the first time I feel guilty since I fucked my husband's assistant. The poor guy thinks I'm jealous when he should be. A familiar scent wafts from behind me, and as I turn around, I see Lara walk by and sit down at our table, right across from me.

The dinner goes by like if I'm watching a movie from outside my body; I can't help being aware of Lara all the time; she acts as if nothing ever happened. I don't notice anything in the looks she gives me from time to time. I have the feeling that I'm indifferent to her sometimes, or is it that she doesn't remember me? Yes, of course, she must remember. The more she ignores me, the more I need her attention. After a couple of glasses of wine, I'm a bit dazed, and I keep remembering everything that happened in that bathroom and the irremediable desire I must repeat it. Could I be a lesbian too? Maybe bisexual? Or is it only Lara that attracts me?

As the minutes pass by, my nervousness grows. I keep heeling my left foot and hemming my napkin as I continue to watch the one who was once my lover. It's been a while since I decided to go and talk to her; I'm just impatiently waiting for the right moment. Lara's passivity makes me desperate, and I need to ask her if we can meet again to chat. However, I'm not sure if it's just talking that I want.

Finally, my moment has arrived, dinner has been over for a while, and now is the time when people start to get up and jump from one table to another with their respective drink in hand, the one that makes you wave and pretend to be excited to see someone you don't even like. As soon as a couple of men assault Alex, I look at Lara and get up to sit next to her. Still, when she sees my intention, she pins her intense gaze on me and stands up, which throws me off and paralyzes me until she starts walking with a determined step in the direction of the restroom. Her attitude makes me doubt. I am not sure if she has avoided me or done it because she wants me to follow her. When in doubt, I choose the option that interests me the most, and I follow her without knowing very well what I am going to tell her.

The walk takes forever, the corridor seems endless, and the heels are killing me. The more steps I take, the more I envy Lara, with her jeans, her jacket, and those flat boots that surely don't squeeze or rub any of her toes. When I finally see the little sign pointing to the bathroom, I sigh with relief, but it doesn't last long. Lara looks at me for a second without stopping walking and passes the bathrooms by. Where is she going? Does she want to torture me? I follow her until we reach the hotel reception. Then she turns down another hallway with more bathrooms and goes inside. I don't know if she's looking for privacy or just doesn't want to be seen talking to me, but I go in after her without really knowing what's going to happen.

When I walk through the door, she has her ass resting on the marble of the sinks, her arms crossed over her chest, and a hard stare that scans and pierces me to my soul.

"Let's get one thing straight," she says without moving, and I would say quite angry, "I would never have hooked up with you if I had known who you were married to."

OK, it's clear that Lara was looking for intimacy, but only to tell me that she thinks I'm a monster. Now it's time to put up with it.

"OK," I mutter in a daze and quite bewildered.

"I can sleep with a married woman; It's not my problem but hers. However, things change if her husband has a face for me, and it changes even more if he's my boss," she continues bellowing, "not to mention that Mr. Ayala is also a good guy."

"I know for a fact that Alex is a good man," I cut her off angrily, "do you think I want to hurt him?"

"The other night in the bathroom, you didn't seem to mind," she says, coming dangerously close with that badass attitude that drives me crazy, "and the way you've been looking at me all through dinner, I'd say you wouldn't mind tonight either," she adds agitated.

I stop her with one hand; she's putting me in a terrible mood.

"You don't know me at all, Lara, don't even think about judging me. There are things that you wouldn't understand and that I can't tell you for now. I'm indeed attracted to you. I want you," I admit.

I notice how her breathing quickens; even the way she looks at me has changed after my confession, she has become more wolfish, but now it's too late.

"Maybe later we can meet for a day and chat if you feel like it."

Lara looks at me, stunned; I don't know what must be going through her head right now. Maybe now she thinks that my husband is not nice to me or something, I hope not. I could tell her that it is only a matter of a short time before I ask my husband for a divorce, but I don't know her. She seems to appreciate Álex, and maybe she'll tell him. I can't allow my husband to find out from someone else before finding out from me; he doesn't deserve it. I must think with my head, control myself, and end this conversation from this moment on. When my life is in order, I know where to find Lara, and it is even possible that I ask her for something like a date. I hope she accepts, but for now, my meeting with her can't go beyond this conversation. And to think that all this happened to me for daring.

Lightning Source UK Ltd.
Milton Keynes UK
UKHW041149160223
417122UK00007BA/934

9 798215 057032